Prais... r Boy Saves Mars

"Deft stimulus for both brains and funny bones."

—Kirkus Reviews

"Kids will roar for *Dinosaur Boy Saves Mars*... Oakes twists her tale with almost-possible plotlines that will appeal perfectly to young SF fans; they'll be stomping around for even more from Sawyer, Sylvie, and Elliot."

—Las Vegas Review

Praise for *Dinosaur Boy*

2016–2017 Florida Sunshine State Young Reader's Award Nominee

Junior Library Guild Pick

"A series debut with more twists than a strand of DNA...good fun."

—Kirkus Reviews

"A fun mix of school drama, science fiction, and humor."

—Booklist

"And you thought your day at school was rough. *Dinosaur Boy* is a hilarious adventure and as sharp as a stegosaurus's tail, with twists and turns on every page… Fantastic."

—Nathan Bransford, author of *Jacob Wonderbar and the Cosmic Space Kapow*

"Filled with depth and emotion I never saw coming. With issues like bullying, not fitting in, and heroism… It's *Wonder* with dinosaurs and is sure to touch your heart."

—P. J. Hoover, author of *Tut: The Story of My Immortal Life*

"A wild and wacky adventure…sure to appeal to wonderfully weird kids of every shape and size."

—Kelly Milner Halls, award-winning author of *In Search of Sasquatch* and *Dinosaur Mummies*

"Dinosaur-human hybrids and mysterious visitors from Mars! What more needs to be said? A delightfully zany and terrifically fun story of friendship, and how to survive fifth grade with a thagomizer of your very own."

—Greg Leitich Smith, award-winning author of *Chronal Engine* and *Little Green Men at the Mercury Inn*

Also by Cory Putman Oakes

Dinosaur Boy

DINOSAUR BOY SAVES MARS

Cory Putman Oakes

sourcebooks
jabberwocky

Published by Sourcebooks Jabberwocky, an imprint of Sourcebooks, Inc.

P.O. Box 4410, Naperville, Illinois 60567-4410

(630) 961-3900

Fax: (630) 961-2168

www.sourcebooks.com

The Library of Congress has cataloged the hardcover edition as follows:

Names: Oakes, Cory Putman.
Title: Dinosaur boy saves Mars / Cory Putman Oakes.
Description: Naperville, Illinois : Sourcebooks Jabberwocky, [2016] | Sequel
   to: Dinosaur boy. | Summary: After heroically saving his classmates,
   fifth-grader Sawyer's life as a dinosaur-human hybrid has gotten a lot
   easier until Sawyer, Sylvie, who is part Martian, and Elliot head to Mars
   in search of Sylvie's missing dad and discover that Mars is trying to kick
   Pluto out of the solar system.
Identifiers: LCCN 2015027628 | (13 : alk. paper)
Subjects: | CYAC: Stegosaurus--Fiction. | Dinosaurs--Fiction. |
   Friendship--Fiction. | Rescues--Fiction. | Schools--Fiction. |
   Extraterrestrial beings--Fiction. | Mars (Planet)--Fiction.
Classification: LCC PZ7.1.O15 Do 2016 | DDC [Fic]--dc23 LC record available at http://lccn.loc.gov/2015027628

Source of Production: Versa Press, East Peoria, Illinois, USA
Date of Production: September 2016
Run Number: 5007433

Printed and bound in the United States of America.
VP 10 9 8 7 6 5 4 3 2 1

For Hanna, Addison, Hayley, Andrew,
Emma, Madison, and Noah.

"And yet our species is young and curious and brave and shows much promise."

—Carl Sagan

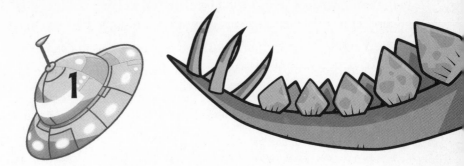

The Jerk

There are lots of cool things about being part stegosaurus.

Trying to get a decent night's sleep isn't one of them.

I used to sleep on my back like a normal person. But now that my back has seventeen hard plates on it, that's no longer an option. Neither is lying on my front, since my back is so heavy that it's hard to breathe when I'm flat on my stomach. Curling up on my side sort of works, but I have to wedge myself into place with tons of pillows so I don't accidentally roll over and squash my plates. And who can sleep when they're practically drowning in pillows?

One night, I even tried to sleep standing up. They say that real stegosauruses might have done that. But real stegosauruses had four legs. I only have two, so let's just say the mechanics didn't exactly work out.

My latest attempt at a comfy sleep position came courtesy of my grandfather. He used to be part stegosaurus himself (until he took the

cure). He told me that when he had dinosaur parts, he never had a good night's sleep either. Until he visited Dubai where he saw a camel kneel in the sand, tuck its legs underneath its body, and take a nap.

I figured it was worth a shot. So last night I got down on all fours in the center of my bed, tucked my knees under my chest, stretched my tail out behind me, and rested my cheek on a stack of pillows.

It must have worked. Or maybe I was just really tired. But either way, I was still in that same position when my mom came in and woke me up early the next morning.

I couldn't figure out why she was telling me I had to get up and go to school. It was a Saturday, after all. And by my count, I still had two days of winter break left.

"It's a makeup day," she explained, waving her phone in my face. I blinked and caught a blurry glimpse of her inbox. "The school is legally required to add an extra day to make up for the ones you missed because of the flooding last month."

"They can just end vacation early like that?" I asked. My dog, Fanny, made an irritated noise from her place at the end of my bed and rolled over, curling herself back into a ball. "On a weekend?"

"I guess so," my mom said. "There's a notice on the school website and they sent an email reminder late last night. We're lucky I didn't miss it!"

"Lucky" wasn't exactly what I was feeling, especially when I caught sight of the bright-yellow assignment sheet on my desk.

"Mom! The paper!"

As homework over break, Ms. Filch had assigned us to figure out what our "passion" was and write a paper about it. I had spent so long staring at the assignment sheet that I now knew the definition of "passion" by heart:

Passion (noun): a strong feeling of enthusiasm or excitement for something or about doing something

I'd spent the entire break trying to figure out a topic, but nothing had come to me. I had gone to bed last night thinking I had two more days for inspiration to strike, but that didn't seem to be true anymore.

My mom patted my tail sympathetically.

"I know you've been trying, Sawyer. I'll write Ms. Filch a note and ask if she'll give you an extension. Now hurry! You don't want to be late for the makeup day!"

As I trudged to school, I tried to put my finger on what was so complicated about figuring out my passion. It wasn't that I didn't have strong feelings about things. Of course I did. There were plenty of things I enjoyed: I liked playing fetch with Fanny; I liked going fishing with my dad; and ever since my herbivore dinosaur gene had kicked in, I really liked salad. But all of those things seemed too boring to be my "passion."

Nobody else seemed to think the assignment was hard. My best friend, Elliot, wrote his paper on basketball. Which made sense, since basketball was hands-down his favorite thing in life.

Our other friend, Sylvie, had so many passions that she outlined three different versions of the paper before she finally decided on the topic, My Hero: My Dad. Sylvie hadn't seen her dad in a while. In fact, she'd been trying to get in touch with him for months now, ever since she first came to our school at the beginning of the year. The whole thing is complicated by the fact that Sylvie's dad is a Martian. So is Sylvie. (Well, a half-Martian since her mom is an Earthling.)

I didn't play any sports. And I didn't have divorced parents who lived on separate planets. So neither of their topics really helped me.

I probably should have just lied and said that I was really passionate about something like stopping global warming. Or Italian food. Ms. Filch probably would have believed either of those. But I would have known it was a lie. And part of me thought it might actually be important to have a passion. I was really annoyed I couldn't think of one.

At least I had my note for Ms. Filch, so I probably wouldn't get in trouble. She'd give me an extension and I could put off worrying about my passion until another day.

But I still had to go to school. On a Saturday. That felt like punishment enough.

A crowd of kids was gathered on the grass in front of the entrance to our school's administration building. It was easy to spot Elliot and Sylvie in the crowd. Elliot, because he was a head taller than everybody else. Sylvie, because her traffic-cone orange sweatshirt made her stick out like a beacon.

"What's going on?" I asked them, double-checking the end of my tail to make sure that all four of my spikes still had a tennis ball skewered onto the tip. My school was fairly strict about that, and I couldn't really blame them. Each of my spikes was a foot long and razor sharp. Without the tennis balls, I was a lethal weapon.

"The school's locked," Elliot answered. "None of the teachers are here."

"That's weird," I said as Sylvie yawned hugely. Her curly brown hair looked even poufier than normal today. Only Elliot and I knew that she did that on purpose to help hide the two antennae she kept pinned tight to her head with barrettes.

"What's weird is that every fifth grader is here, but practically no one else," Sylvie said, waving her hand at the kids standing all around us. She was right. There were a couple of fourth graders and a few sixth graders floating around, but everyone else I could see was in fifth grade like us.

Things got even weirder a couple of minutes later when a car squealed into the parking lot and Principal Kline jumped out. I hardly recognized him at first, probably because he was wearing long shorts, a T-shirt, and flip-flops. He also had a bit of a beard going on, like he hadn't shaved in a couple of weeks.

Not that I'm complaining about Principal Kline. As far as I was concerned, he could wear whatever he wanted as long as he wasn't planning to sell any of my classmates to intergalactic rare pet dealers (like our last principal). But since he almost always wore khakis and collared shirts to school, I was guessing he hadn't planned on coming in that day.

I was right.

"Everyone!" Principal Kline said, commanding our attention from the top step of the administration building. "I'm afraid there's been a mix-up. Last night, an unauthorized user gained access to the school's administrative account and sent an email to all the fifth-grade parents. Our school website was also tampered with. There's no school today. It's not a 'makeup day' or anything like that. Please sit tight while I send out a corrected email and call all of your parents. It might take a while."

"The school got hacked? Who would do that?" Sylvie asked. From all of the chatter going on around us, it was obvious that everyone was asking each other the same thing.

Elliot and I both sighed.

"Orlando must be back," I theorized.

"He's early this year," Elliot pointed out.

"Who's early?" Sylvie asked, crossing her arms. She hated not being the one who figured things out.

I pulled out my phone, but its battery was dead.

"Quick," I said to Elliot. "Check the school Wi-Fi."

Elliot dug his phone out of his pocket. Usually there was only one Wi-Fi network available on school grounds: JACKJAMESELEMENTARY (password: JackJames). Now there was still only one. But its name was: ORLANDOTOTALLYROCKS.

"Yeah, that's usually the first thing he does," I said.

"Who's Orlando?" Sylvie asked.

"Orlando Eris," I told her. "He's in our class, but you haven't met him yet because he lives in San Diego with his dad for the first half of every year. He only comes home to Portland after winter break."

"Orlando's obsessed with practical jokes," Elliot added. "He even runs a blog. See?"

He angled his phone so Sylvie and I both had a perfect view of a website called Prankster King Orlando. Beneath the obnoxious red title and a big cartoon crown was today's blog entry: a live-stream video of the front of a school, with dozens of kids gathered on the lawn.

It was us. Orlando was live streaming a video of us.

"That jerk!"

The shout came from Allan Huxley, who was also looking down at his phone. Until recently, Allan had been my greatest enemy at school. But we had come to an understanding after Sylvie and I saved him (and a good portion of the rest of our class) from taking a one-way trip to Jupiter. It's kind of a long story, and we still weren't exactly friends, but Allan and I had managed to coexist in relative peace for quite some time now. He hadn't called me Butt Brain in three months and counting.

But hearing him yell like that still sent a chill down my plates.

As if on cue, the video feed paused and a picture of Orlando popped up in front of it. He looked exactly like I remembered him from last year: a black-haired, pasty-skinned kid in big glasses. He grinned at the camera and slowly held up a sign.

DID YOU MISS ME?

"Jerk!" Allan yelled again. Without warning, he started running toward a Dumpster on the edge of the grass, just as a small, bespectacled figure with a video camera in one hand darted out from behind it.

Principal Kline took off after them about a second later, running awkwardly in his flip-flops. Most of our class members, including Elliot and Sylvie, started cheering Allan on at the top of their lungs.

But I didn't. I was too busy thinking a rather out-of-place and very annoying thought: Orlando Eris may have been a jerk, but at least he had a passion. He probably wouldn't have any trouble writing his paper.

The Glue Incident

Orlando's "makeup day" stunt got him suspended for three days. I'm pretty sure he spent the entire time thinking up new prank ideas, because when he finally returned to school he had a new practical joke planned for every day.

On his first day back, he deflated all the volleyballs in the gym.

The second day, he put birdseed on top of all the cars in the faculty parking lot. The picture on his blog that night was a close-up of Principal Kline's car covered in bird poop.

The day after that, he released a jar of crickets into a loose ceiling panel in the boys' bathroom. They spread all over the school. Now, whenever it gets quiet in a classroom, we can hear them chirping above our heads.

Unlike the Wi-Fi thing, there was no actual proof he did any of those things. But everybody knew it was him. It was always him. You only had to read his blog to know.

He was pretty much permanently in detention, but he didn't seem to care. And he didn't have any friends, but he didn't seem to mind that either.

I'm not sure if his lack of friends was the reason he pulled so many pranks. Or if pulling so many pranks was the reason for his lack of friends. It didn't really matter. The end result was the same. Every day, Orlando ate lunch by himself at the center of an otherwise empty cafeteria table. Like there was some kind of invisible force field between him and everybody else at school.

Most of the stuff he did was more annoying than harmful. Like rearranging all the desks in our homeroom to face backward. Or taking a selfie and setting it as the background on Ms. Filch's computer. Or gluing the caps onto all of Ms. Filch's pens. He really seemed to like tormenting Ms. Filch. She was pretty patient with him, considering. Until the day that Orlando put superglue all over her chair right before free reading period.

By the end of free reading period, Ms. Filch's jeans were permanently attached to the chair. We all had to leave the room while another female teacher came to help her get out of them. And to hold a towel around her until someone could find something else for her to wear. Orlando got a picture of the janitor hauling away Ms. Filch's ruined chair (with her jeans still attached) and put it up on his blog. And Instagram. It got three thousand likes in less than an hour.

That was when Ms. Filch kind of lost it.

At lunch that day, she made us all sit at our desks and explained that we would not be allowed to leave the room until someone confessed to being the glue perpetrator.

"Ms. Filch?" Elliot called out from the back row, waving one of his long, skinny arms in the air. "Why do we all have to sit here? Everybody knows that it was—"

Ms. Filch raised a hand to silence him.

"I don't care if you know who it was, Elliot. I don't care if everybody in this room knows. It's not just about who did it. I said I want a confession. A confession is about taking responsibility. And until someone confesses, the entire class will eat their lunch at their desks. Silently."

We all turned to glare at Orlando.

He pushed a strand of hair off his forehead, adjusted his glasses, and started unwrapping his sandwich. He looked exactly the way he always did at lunch: small, quiet, and completely unbothered. And not like someone who was about to take responsibility for anything.

We all took out our lunches. I poured dressing over my favorite salad (mixed greens, tomatoes, cucumbers, and banana peppers) and as I ate, I stared at the first page of my notebook where I had started a brainstorming list for my "passion" paper.

So far, the list consisted of the words "Possible Passions," underlined twice, with nothing underneath.

At the desk next to me, Sylvie pushed back the hood of her sweatshirt and nodded to my notebook.

"What's that for?" she whispered.

"I still have to write my paper," I whispered back. Ms. Filch had given me a two-week extension. But I still had no idea what I was going to write about.

"Oh that," Sylvie said, unwrapping a pack of Starburst. "I got an A-minus on mine."

"For a Martian, you're really good at English," I grumbled, taking a big bite of my salad.

"Oh, not especially," Sylvie said, sandwiching a pink Starburst between two yellow ones and biting them in half. "All Martians speak English."

"Really?" I asked. "That seems weird."

"Why?" Sylvie asked, lowering her voice to an even quieter, mysterious tone. "Who do you think taught it to you Earthlings?"

"Really?" I said again, louder this time.

"Shhh!" Ms. Filch hissed from the front of the room.

We were both quiet for a minute. When Ms. Filch returned to her book, Sylvie leaned toward me again.

"Actually, it's because Martians are obsessed with American TV," she confessed. "All the planets are. My dad says nothing has united the galaxy like everybody's shared love for *American Idol*. They speak English at all important intergalactic summits now. It's very trendy."

"Huh," I said thoughtfully.

I returned to my notebook and wrote "TV" as the first item on my list.

I crossed it off a second later, after I remembered I hardly ever watched TV. There had to be something I was more passionate about than that.

Lunch seemed to take a lot longer than usual. By the time the bell finally rang, I had eaten my entire salad and had written and crossed out three more items on my list. Sylvie had ripped her Starburst wrappers into tiny pieces and used them to spell out *ORLANDO SUCKS* across her desk. At the back of the room, Elliot had his legs stretched out in the aisle, his head tilted over the back of his chair, and was taking what looked like the world's most uncomfortable nap.

Ms. Filch got up from her desk and gave Orlando a pointed look. He pushed his glasses farther up his nose and blinked at her.

Ms. Filch sighed. "It looks like we'll all be having lunch together tomorrow too."

The UFO

We had lunch inside every day for the next week. Ms. Filch refused to back down and Orlando refused to confess. I had just begun to think I would be spending every lunch period for the rest of fifth grade at my desk when finally, the following Tuesday, Ms. Filch was forced to let us outside.

It wasn't because Orlando confessed. It was because the school had finally decided to do something about the crickets, and the stuff the pest-control people sprayed inside the school was supposed to dissipate for an hour before any of us breathed it. So my class got to join the rest of the school in the courtyard during lunchtime.

I had just finished my salad. I was standing around with Elliot and Sylvie, enjoying the feel of the sun on my plates, when all of a sudden a tornado-level wind whipped up and knocked over every trash can in sight. Garbage scattered everywhere and some of the smaller kids had to grab on to bigger ones so they wouldn't get blown away too.

Everyone was staring up at the sky and pointing. I craned my dinosaur neck at a painful angle so that I could see the large, circular object that was hovering over the quad and blocking out the sun.

The disk just hung there for a split second, like a humongous spinning quarter. Then the wind stopped and it fell to the ground with a deafening crash. Pieces of asphalt went flying in all directions, and roughly half the kids standing nearby were knocked off their feet. It was a miracle that no one got flattened.

The UFO did take out three of the four outdoor basketball hoops on its way down. But nobody seemed to notice because as soon as the disk stopped spinning, a small door opened on the underside and two enormous polar bears came charging down the gangplank.

The bears tore through the crowd, making weird, trumpetlike sounds and knocking kids aside like bowling pins. The panic was total. Everybody, including me, scrambled, trying to find a safe direction to run in. But whenever I managed to get myself out of the path of one of the bears, I instantly found myself right in front of the other one. So I ended up huddled between Elliot and Sylvie, smashed in a shaky clump with a large group of other fifth graders.

Eventually the bears stopped running and started pacing. They made slow circles around us, clicking their long, black claws against the cracked asphalt and holding their noses high. The larger of the two passed within a foot of me. It was sniffing the air in an expectant way. Exactly like Fanny does when my mom cooks bacon.

Which made me wonder if perhaps we were the bacon in this scenario.

But before I could get too worried about it, another figure appeared on the UFO gangplank. It was not another polar bear. It was a man—a rugged-looking, gray-haired man wearing a leather Indiana Jones hat and jeans. He raised his fingers to his lips and let out a shrill whistle.

The polar bears stopped dead in their tracks. Then they lowered their heads and backed away, just like Fanny does when she's caught misbehaving. When they were about ten feet away from the mass of students, they both sat down on their hindquarters so that they strongly resembled enormous, salivating teddy bears.

My grandfather lowered his fingers from his mouth and shouted, *"Who's got the peanut butter?"*

Nobody answered him, so my grandfather repeated the question as he came toward us.

"Who's got the peanut butter?"

I heard mutterings of confusion in the huddled mass of kids around me, but nothing resembling a response until Gary Simmons timidly cleared his throat and raised his hand.

"Yes?" my grandfather called on him, impatiently.

"Um, well, sir," Gary stammered. "We're actually a nut-free campus."

"A what?"

"Nut-free. Be-be-because so many people have allergies."

My grandfather blinked at him for a moment, then shook his head resolutely.

"Nope. Somebody has peanut butter. Otherwise, they wouldn't have acted like that." He motioned to the polar bears. They were still frozen in teddy-bear poses, which would have been funny if we weren't all still shaking so badly.

My grandfather narrowed his eyes, just as Emma Hecht pushed past me and took a step forward.

"It's me," she admitted, looking horribly ashamed as she handed my grandfather a pink Hello Kitty lunch sack. "My grandma packed my lunch this morning. She never remembers the rule about nuts. I'm sorry."

My grandfather opened the sack and pulled out a plastic bag, which contained a slightly smushed, crustless peanut-butter-and-jelly sandwich cut into triangles.

The polar bears both sat forward eagerly.

"I never even took it out of the bag," Emma said hurriedly. "Just in case."

"That was smart of you," my grandfather said and gave her a reassuring smile as he tossed the sandwich toward the bears. Each one caught a triangle in midair and gulped it down. Then they sat back on their haunches, smacking their lips with long, black tongues.

My grandfather cleared his throat.

"No harm done," he said to Emma, and then he raised his voice so that even the kids in the back of the crowd could hear. "But let this be a lesson to all of you. If you don't respect the dietary restrictions of your fellow classmates, the polar bears will come back. Got it?"

There was a smattering of mmm-hmms, yeses, and nods. But basically everybody just continued to stare at him.

My grandfather nodded smartly, finally spotted me in the crowd, and grinned.

"Ah, Sawyer," he said. Then he noticed Sylvie and Elliot standing beside me. "And Sylvia, good. And also…also…"

He frowned for a moment over Elliot's name.

"Elliot," Elliot reminded him.

"Of course, Elliot," he said, as he handed Emma back her empty lunch sack. "Glad to see you. I came here looking for the three of you."

"You did?" I asked, feeling rather awkward. Emma slipped back behind me, holding her lunch sack protectively to her chest.

"Yes. I'm afraid Sylvie's father may be in trouble. I'm going to need your help."

Elliot and I just stood there dumbly. But Sylvie let out an enormous sigh of relief.

"Finally," she muttered. Then she slung her enormous lunch bag over her shoulder and walked up the gangplank of the ship, right past my grandfather, without looking back once to see if Elliot and I were coming.

My grandfather grinned down at me.

"Well? Are you ready for an adventure or what?"

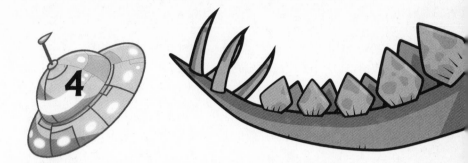

Extinction and Stuff

The UFO was smaller on the inside than it had looked from the outside. But even though it wasn't very big, there seemed to be a lot of empty space. The interior was a circular room that had absolutely nothing in it except leather armchairs. They encircled the ship's only window, which happened to be in the middle of the floor.

When Elliot and I got onboard, Sylvie was already sitting cross-legged in one of the chairs, drumming her fingers on the armrest.

My grandfather came in behind us. He shut the door behind the polar bears and took the seat next to Sylvie.

I frowned at the nearest chair. It was one of those squishy leather recliners, and there was no opening for my tail to go through the back. There was also no seat belt, which I suppose meant we didn't necessarily have to sit in chairs. With a questioning glance at my grandfather—who nodded OK—I took a seat on the floor next to the window.

My grandfather picked up an iPad and pressed a button. There was a slight whirring sound, a metallic groan from somewhere deep in the wall, and then a sensation like we had just stepped into a high-speed elevator.

Elliot sat down to my right, and his eyes got as big as saucers as we both stared out the window and watched the quad, then the school, then Portland, and then the entire state of Oregon disappear beneath us.

One of the polar bears lumbered over and dropped to the floor on my other side. I stiffened, and my tail spikes gave an instinctive twitch. Ready to do…I don't know what. But the bear just stretched out its paws and leaned its large, shaggy head out over the window, fogging up the glass with its peanut butter breath. I might have been imagining things, but I thought the enormous, brown eye closest to me looked sad.

The other bear was lying on the floor behind Sylvie's chair, its head on its paws and its eyes closed. Both bears seemed much calmer after eating Emma's sandwich. But even so, I made sure my tennis-balled spikes were within easy reach of my hand.

"We've got one stop to make before we deal with Sylvie's dad," my grandfather said. He looked up from his iPad. That must be what he was using to fly the ship. I couldn't imagine how else we were moving. There wasn't a control panel, a wall of buttons, or anything remotely electronic anywhere. The curved, wood-paneled walls all around us made the room look more like my family's summer cabin than a spaceship.

The door and the gangplank had disappeared behind one of the panels as soon as the four of us and the two bears had gotten inside. I had lost track of where it had disappeared. Something about the room being a circle made me lose my sense of direction.

"A stop?" Sylvie asked, sounding irritated. She sat forward, shook her hood off, and gave my grandfather a severe look. "Where? Why are we stopping?"

"Saturn," my grandfather answered and gestured to the polar bears as though that should explain everything. "We've got to drop these guys off."

"On Saturn?" Elliot exclaimed with a dubious look at the bears. "I thought Saturn was made out of gas."

"Just the outer layers," my grandfather assured him, then started feeling around his seat as though he had dropped something. "Has anyone seen my Snickers bar? I could have sworn I left it here when we landed."

Sylvie turned to Elliot and me. "Saturn is a game preserve," she explained. "Kind of like a big zoo, but fancier."

"You've been to Saturn?" I asked, not knowing quite why I was surprised.

"Oh yeah," Sylvie said, like it was no big deal. "We used to go there all the time on school field trips."

Elliot shook his head, as he often did after one of Sylvie's especially odd pronouncements.

"So we're bringing the polar bears to a zoo on Saturn?" I summed up, just to make sure I had it right.

"Yes," my grandfather answered. As he spoke, he searched the empty chairs around the circle, still looking for his candy bar. "The bears are part of the Amalgam Labs Extinction Eradication project.

When a species in our galaxy arrives at the brink of extinction, our lab recruits two volunteers, one male and one female of the species, and relocates them to Saturn. There they enjoy a pampered life in a simulated habitat while we can be sure that their genetic material will be preserved."

"And we have to do that now?" Sylvie inquired, sounding antsy.

"This ship belongs to the lab," my grandfather explained. "I needed a legitimate, scientific purpose to bring her out. Listen, are you sure you're not sitting on my candy bar? I know I—"

"Will it take long to drop them off?" Sylvie pressed him, ignoring his question.

The polar bear beside me snorted, and Elliot and I both jumped.

"So sorry to be a bother," the bear said. "We had no idea that the predicted extinction of our entire species would be such a massive inconvenience for you all."

◆◆◆

Neither Sylvie nor my grandfather appeared to be alarmed (or even surprised) that a polar bear had just spoken to us. Let alone sarcastically and in a voice that sounded like it belonged to somebody's English grandmother.

Elliot and I were not nearly so cool about it.

"You—you, you can talk?" Elliot squealed, scrambling behind me and using me as a shield as we both backed away. "In English?"

"Yes, I speak English. Also Finnish," the bear bragged.

"Big whoop," Sylvie said from safely over on her chair.

The bear whipped her head toward Sylvie and made a growling noise in the back of her throat. I scooted back some more, bumped into Elliot, and motioned for him to scoot back more too.

"Harriet," scolded the other bear from over beside Sylvie's chair. He—his voice had sounded male—raised his head ever so slightly and yawned without opening his eyes. "Do try to keep it together."

"Well, I'm sorry, Roland," the bear next to me retorted, sitting back on her haunches in much the same manner as she had after my grandfather whistled. "But I still have very mixed feelings about this whole thing."

"What?" My grandfather looked up suddenly. "I was told you had both been fully briefed and signed all of the necessary paper—"

"We have and we did," the male polar bear—Roland—assured him, rolling lazily onto one side. "Harriet is just having an attack of nostalgia. Aren't you, dear?"

Harriet gave him a look. It clearly said, "Don't you *dear* me," in polar bear. Or possibly Finnish. Then she snorted and looked back down at the portal window. Which, I realized suddenly, had gotten much darker. The Earth was now a small orb, no bigger than a basketball floating in a sea of black.

"Wow," I said, deciding to risk creeping slightly closer to the bear so I could see out the window better.

"Good-bye, home," Harriet said wistfully, and I felt a sudden stab of pity for her. I wanted to do something to make her feel better. But I was not at all sure how to go about comforting a homesick polar bear.

Sylvie cleared her throat.

"Can we get back to my father, please?" she asked testily. She turned to my grandfather. "You said you think he's in trouble?"

"Yes," my grandfather said, picking up his iPad again. "I believe he may have been kidnapped."

Gloria

K idnapped?" Sylvie sounded unconvinced. "Who would kidnap him?"

My grandfather started to turn the iPad screen toward Sylvie, then hesitated.

His face softened. And for once he looked more like a grandpa than a scientist. Or Indiana Jones. He put his hand on top of Sylvie's.

"I don't want to upset you," he told her.

Sylvie stuck her nose in the air.

"It's my father we're talking about. I need to know what's happened to him."

My grandfather considered this, then nodded slowly and patted her hand.

"When you told me, months ago, that you hadn't heard from him since you got to Earth, I got suspicious. So I convinced Amalgam Labs to start monitoring all communications coming from Mars. Recently, we intercepted an interesting series of transmissions. Most were scientific in nature. But we found one snippet we believe might be a distress signal sent by your father."

"How do you know it's from him?" Sylvie asked.

My grandfather handed her the iPad.

"It's incomplete," he warned, and Elliot and I came over so that we could see too. "Most of the file has been corrupted, so we only have pieces."

```
Gloria
A*(798H FSKJHF89 FHSDOFj
LK(*   hJK   *(&#   being   held
against my will FHKF 8F*(&(
FSkk 2 kjfu4
Tell Sylvie not to *(&*(SFKH
290HJKHK
(&)(Jkhkjh @GHJGJH &F(HJK#
```

"Who's Gloria?" Elliot asked, peering over Sylvie's shoulder.

"My mom," she answered. Her voice sounded a little shaky, but her eyes were steely when she looked up at my grandfather.

"Who's holding my father against his will?" she asked.

"We believe it's Sunder Labs," my grandfather answered. "Amalgam Lab's greatest rival. Until about a year ago, they were based out of Houston, Texas. But then they ran into money problems and abandoned their campus there. We—Amalgam Labs, that is—suspect that they have reestablished a secret base on Mars, where land is cheaper. But no one has been able to find it yet. We believe their new lab is the source of these transmissions."

"And you think my father is there?" Sylvie asked.

My grandfather nodded. "Yes. As soon as we drop the polar bears off, we're headed to Mars."

Sylvie nodded, seemingly in agreement with this plan, as she handed the iPad back to my grandfather. Out of the corner of my eye, I caught sight of Roland, still lounging behind Sylvie's chair.

The big bear had opened his eyes.

"Why would a laboratory kidnap Sylvie's dad?" I asked. "I thought he owned a bunch of restaurants."

Roland rolled to his feet, nose in the air. Over by the portal, Harriet's nose was also twitching.

"In addition to being a restaurateur, Asaph Juarez is the Chancellor in Charge of Martian-Human Affairs," my grandfather reminded me, watching as the polar bears began a slow circuit of the ship, industriously sniffing each wood panel in turn. "Mars has a delicate political situation at the moment. It's possible Sylvie's dad got caught in the middle of it."

"Political situation?" I repeated.

"Just local politics," he said as Roland and Harriet lingered in front of a nondescript piece of wall, almost directly across the ship from where I was crouched beside Sylvie's chair. "Nothing to do with us."

"Asaph Juarez?" Elliot said thoughtfully, looking at Sylvie. "I thought that was your mom's last name."

"It is," Sylvie said. She was watching the bears too. Roland was now standing on his hind legs, his front paws braced against the panel.

"Yeah, but aren't they…well, divorced?" Elliot asked. "Why didn't your mom change her name back to what it was before she married your dad?"

"Juarez was my mom's name," Sylvie informed him. "In Mars, when you get married, the guy takes the girl's last name."

"You mean *on* Mars?" Elliot said, smirking.

"No, Elliot. How many times do I have to tell you? When you're talking about Mars, you always say—"

But she was interrupted when Roland raised a paw and ripped a rectangular section of wood paneling right off the wall. A smell, like a combination of sauerkraut and dirty socks, filled the air. There was a small yelp of surprise, and Roland and Harriet both backed out of the way as something fell out of the wall.

It froze in place, hanging strangely out of the hidden cabinet with its head on the floor and its legs sticking up in the air. It was about Sylvie's size, maybe a bit smaller. But this was no Martian. Most of its body was covered in a skin-tight, black bodysuit. But the parts that were sticking out—its hands, feet, and head—were all a faint shade of blue.

It was clutching a half-eaten Snickers bar in one of its hands.

By the time I got to my feet, my grandfather was already over by the panel, pointing a large, silver revolver at the creature's head.

"Freeze, BURPSer," he said icily.

The Stowaway

I couldn't stop staring at the gun in my grandfather's hand. It was shiny and metallic and had swirly designs etched all over it. The handle was ivory and it had a spinning chamber for the bullets. It looked like the kind of thing you'd see in the Old West, in the hands of a grizzly old sheriff. But definitely not on a spaceship.

The creature was staring at the gun too.

"I am not a BURPSer," it said indignantly.

"On your feet," my grandfather ordered in the same scary tone.

As commanded, the creature executed an awkward (and, frankly, quite painful-looking) wiggle that brought its legs down out of the cupboard. As soon as it had its feet on the floor, it raised both hands, including the one still holding the Snickers bar, over its head and stood to its full height. Which brought it roughly to my chin.

It was built like a human: two arms, two legs, and so on. He— because now that he was upright, I could tell he was a he—probably could have passed for a human, although a short one, if he hadn't been blue. His hair was bright blond and stuck straight up out of his head. There was a chocolate smear on his chin, and he smelled very strongly of the odor that had preceded him out of the cupboard. His gray eyes grew very wide as Roland took a step closer.

The blue kid—he looked about my age, but it was hard to tell with all of the blue—threw the half-eaten candy bar so it landed right in front of the polar bear. Roland picked up the bar, gestured to Harriet, and the two of them retreated a short distance away to enjoy their snack.

The creature raised his hands back to surrender position and then gulped when he saw that my grandfather was still holding the gun on him.

"I am not a BURPSer," he repeated.

"Prove it," my grandfather ordered.

"My name is Venetio Lowell, um, sir," he said, pronouncing his name like Ven-ee-shee-O. "The ship I, er, borrowed is very old and I got trapped in Earth's orbit so I hitched a ride on yours to get me going again, and wow..." He caught sight of me, and his eyes grew even wider. "Um, what are you?"

"I'm not a what," I told him, bristling slightly. I was used to people doing a double take when they saw my plates and my tail, but this tiny, blue person hardly seemed in a position to be startled by it. "I'm a who. I'm Sawyer."

"Course—course you are!" Venetio said with an attempt at a laugh. He glanced nervously over at the polar bears for a moment, then back to my grandfather. "I really do apologize for sneaking onboard, sir. But I'd been drifting for days and days, and yours was the only craft I saw, so I didn't have much of a choice."

"You're a stowaway?" Elliot asked, sounding thrilled by the idea.

"Er, yeah, I suppose so," Venetio said, with a shrug of apology. "But only because of dire necessity. I'm no BURPSer!"

"But you are a thief," my grandfather pointed out, nodding over at the bears, who were licking chocolate off their paws.

"I didn't mean to take it," Venetio said sadly as his stomach growled. "But I ran out of food, and when you left the ship, it was just sitting there on your chair…" He trailed off, looking vaguely ashamed, then drew himself up straight. "But I am not a BURPSer!"

"What is a 'burpser'?" I finally asked. And in spite of the tension of the room, I distinctively heard Elliot stifle a giggle. "I mean, it's not what it sounds like, is it?"

"'BURPS' stands for 'Brotherhood United for the Restoration of Planetary Status,'" my grandfather explained. "Its members are called BURPSers. They are a radical Plutonian organization that formed after Pluto was reclassified as a dwarf planet."

"Oh, B-U-R-P-S." Elliot puzzled out, then guffawed. "Ha! That's funny!"

Nobody else laughed.

"Actually, after they figured out what their name spelled, they changed it to 'the Plutonian Restoration Society.' The 'PRS,'" Venetio put in. "The old name kind of stuck though. But I am not one of them."

"You are quite obviously a Plutonian," my grandfather pointed out. "What are you doing so far from home?"

"I was bound for Mars, sir. But like I said, I had some trouble with my ship, so I attached to yours and climbed in through one of your service panels. I was only going to stay long enough to maybe, er, borrow a bit of fuel. But then I heard you tell one of the polar bears you were headed to Mars, so I thought I might just stay—"

"In the cupboard?" my grandfather cut in.

Venetio shrugged.

"It's a good deal more comfortable than my ship, sir."

He smiled affably at each of us in turn, and I found it hard not to smile back.

"Um, can I put my hands down now?" he asked.

"If you're not a BURPSer," my grandfather pressed him, ignoring his request, "then why are you trying to get to Mars?"

"Why? Why else? For the game!"

"What game?" my grandfather asked.

Moving very slowly, the Plutonian lowered one hand, reached into the breast pocket of his bodysuit, and pulled out a folded piece of paper the size of an index card.

"Sawyer," my grandfather said. "Check it out."

I took a deep breath and approached the Plutonian, trying to act like I assisted my grandfather in holding aliens at gunpoint every day. When I got close enough to take the ticket out of his hand, I saw beads of sweat collected on his blueish forehead.

"Can I please put my hands down?" Venetio repeated and looked quite relieved when my grandfather nodded.

The ticket said:

ADMIT 1	THE 2016 SUMMIT FRIENDSHIP AND GOODWILL GAME
Section 8, Row 95, Seat 34C	MARS'S RED RAZERS vs. PLUTO'S KUIPER KICKERS

The term "Red Razer" seemed vaguely familiar, but I couldn't place it.

"The rematch!" Venetio exclaimed, looking very excited. "You know, Pluto versus Mars? It's the first time we've played the Razers since the '14 Finals!"

I heard Sylvie draw in a breath. She stepped up behind me and peered over my shoulder at the ticket.

"How did you get this?" she asked, and I was surprised at the coldness in her voice. And the very particular way that she said the word "you."

"I won it!" Venetio said proudly, narrowing his eyes at Sylvie. They were almost exactly the same height. "From a radio station. I correctly named all of the Kuiper Kicker strikers who have ever scored goals in intergalactic tournaments."

"All of them?" Elliot asked.

"Well, there aren't really that many," Venetio admitted. "We don't score that often. But I really think this could be our year! If—"

"That's why you're here?" my grandfather interrupted, lowering the gun ever so slightly. "For the game? It's nothing to do with the summit?"

"The summit?" I asked, as Venetio shook his head vigorously.

"I'm not interested in politics, sir. I'm just here for my team."

He unzipped the front of his suit to reveal a well-worn jersey with *K2! KUIPER KICKERS!* emblazoned on the front.

My grandfather lowered his gun slightly.

"How old are you?" he asked. "And where did you get your ship? You said you borrowed it?"

"I'm eleven," Venetio answered. Then he gritted his teeth. "The ship belongs to my mom. She's going to kill me when I get home. But it'll be worth it. This is a once-in-a-lifetime game, and I just can't miss it, sir. You understand?"

My grandfather lowered his gun completely.

"All right, Venetio," he said. "We'll bring you along. Call your mother and tell her you're OK. But if you cause any trouble—"

"I won't," the Plutonian assured him. Then he turned to me and held out his hand. "My ticket please?"

After a nod from my grandfather, I handed it back to him.

Venetio cupped it briefly in his hands, then folded it reverently and placed it back inside his breast pocket. He smiled at all of us again. I went to smile back, but found that I couldn't. A chill had come over me.

I had just remembered why the name "Red Razers" was familiar.

It was the name of the Martian soccer team. And the last time I had seen it, it had been written on a key chain. A key chain that held the key to the portable classroom where Principal Mathis had kept twelve of my classmates, including Elliot, prisoner. Until Sylvie and I had rescued them.

A second chill came over me. I did my best to shake it off as Venetio turned and settled himself into one of the leather armchairs.

"Ahhhh," he said, closing his eyes. "Much more comfortable than the cupboard."

Not the Twilight Zone

My grandfather had to put down the gun to pick up his iPad, but it was still within easy reach on the seat next to him.

He caught me looking at it and grinned.

"Not exactly what you were expecting to see on a spaceship, I suppose?" he asked.

"I guess not," I said. Although after the polar bears and the surprise Plutonian, I wasn't sure what I expected anymore.

My grandfather picked up the gun and twirled it around his hand once like a gunfighter.

"It may not be cutting edge," he admitted, tucking it into his pants, just underneath the back flap of his jacket. "But it does the trick. I've done some cool modifications on it. Plus, it qualifies as an 'historical artifact' as opposed to a 'weapon,' so it's much easier to travel with."

"What's the 'summit'?" I asked suddenly. "You asked Venetio if that was why he was going to Mars. What is it?"

My grandfather waved his hand dismissively in the air.

"Oh, that's what I was referring to when I mentioned the local politics," he explained. "It's just a bunch of Martian politicians getting together to decide on something. Very boring. Nothing for you to worry about. But there's always a lot of media at these kinds of events and the Plutonians, especially the BURPSers, like to use these occasions to make a stink. Just to remind us all that they're still sore about being considered a dwarf planet."

I gave our stowaway a sideways glance.

"Are they dangerous? The BURPSers, I mean."

"Well…" My grandfather considered this, as he scratched the back of his neck. "They did try to blow up Neptune once. It didn't work," he added hastily as Elliot walked up to us.

"Um, Dr. Franklin, how long before we get to Saturn?" he inquired. He looked excited. And because I know him so well, I could practically see every *Twilight Zone* episode running through his brain at once. "Will we have to go into cryogenetic freeze? Will time go by faster on Earth so we can meet our great-great-grandkids when we get home? How do we go to the bathroom? Will we have to do exercises to counteract the effect that prolonged zero gravity has on muscles?"

"We should arrive in about eight minutes," my grandfather told him gently. "So we probably don't have to worry about, well, most of those things."

"Oh," said Elliot, looking deflated.

"But the bathroom's just over there if you need it," my grandfather added, pointing to the wall directly behind us. It looked like all of the other wood-paneled curves, except that it had a male-female sign on it, just like the ones on our bathrooms at school.

"Oh," said Elliot.

Looking massively disappointed by the normalcy of it all, he set off toward the bathroom door.

I was still not willing to try to cram my dinosaur butt into one of the chairs. So I sat back down at my spot on the floor by the window. Harriet was there too. And when she noticed me shifting around on the floor, trying to find a more comfortable position for my tail, she moved over a little bit, giving me room to spread out my four tennis-balled spikes.

"Thanks," I said.

She grunted. Earth was no longer visible in the window, but her eyes remained locked on the dark portal all the same. They looked sad again.

"So polar bears are going extinct?" I asked. Then I swallowed, worried that this wasn't exactly light conversation.

"Apparently so," she said with a sigh. "Our numbers have been dwindling for some time, along with the ice, so I can't say that I'm shocked."

"Hmmm," I said thoughtfully, recalling the Amalgam Labs video I had been forced to watch in homeroom at the beginning of this year. How many dinosaur-human hybrids had Dr. Dana said there were? Several dozen? That wasn't very many. I wondered if that meant I was endangered. Or possibly headed for extinction myself.

"I'm sorry," I told her, meaning it. "That totally stinks."

"Yes, it does."

After a moment's pause, the polar bear spoke again.

"Thank you for saying that. Most people... Well, let's just say that most people don't care about anything unless it's personal to them. That's the whole problem with being endangered, you see. No one takes it personally until it's too late, and by then, there aren't enough of us left to do anything about it."

"I can see the problem," I muttered. "Um, can all polar bears talk?"

I couldn't resist asking, even though I suspected it might make Harriet mad. So I was relieved when she cocked her head to one side and gave me the nearest possible thing to a polar bear smile.

"Of course we can, love. It's just that we have so little to say to humans."

A few minutes later, we landed on the roof of Noah Station 2 on Saturn.

A shuttle was waiting to take Harriet and Roland to the northern part of the planet. Where, my grandfather said, the simulated Arctic Circle environment would be perfect for the bears.

My grandfather went down the gangplank to talk to the shuttle pilot, while Harriet and Roland climbed lumberously to their feet and stretched.

"Good-bye, dear," Harriet said to me, and I thought she sounded a bit more cheerful than she had a few minutes ago.

"Good-bye, Harriet," I said, fighting a very strong urge to give her a hug.

She and Roland were halfway down the ramp when Sylvie ran after them.

"Wait!" she called. As she ran, she dug one hand around in the front pocket of her sweatshirt. When her hand emerged, it was clutching a fistful of partially melted Reese's Peanut Butter Cups.

She put the candy into one of Harriet's hairy paws.

"I told you I smelled something," Roland growled.

Harriet breathed in the smell of the treat with a satisfied grunt.

"Thank you, Sylvie," she said. "I do hope you find your father."

"I hope you like your new planet," Sylvie said back.

Moments later, we blasted off. From the portal window, I watched Noah Station 2 and the surrounding forest fall away. And I thought I saw a small, crested head on the end of a long, gray dinosaur neck rise gracefully above a clump of greenery to watch us fly away.

But I might have been imagining things.

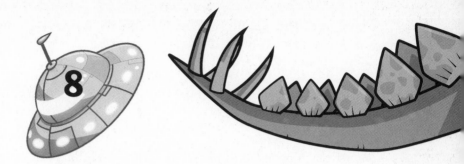

Sushi in Space

Eighteen minutes to Mars orbit," my grandfather said cheerfully.

I was finally sitting on one of the chairs. I had to perch on the very edge to avoid smashing my plates against the back and to allow my tail to curve over the front. But my butt, which had fallen asleep after sitting on the floor for so long, was much more comfortable now.

I hadn't had any warning that I'd be taking a trip to Mars that day, so I didn't have much stuff with me. Just my lunch sack (with the remains of my lunch inside), my notebook, and a pen. I opened the notebook and added "Preventing the Extinction of Polar Bears" to my Possible Passions list.

"Is that for your paper?" Elliot asked, reading over my shoulder. "You got the extension?"

I nodded.

"I got a B minus on mine," Elliot said and flopped into the chair next to mine. "Ms. Filch doesn't think basketball is a good enough passion. She told me I needed to 'dig deeper.'"

"Hmmm," I said and frowned down at my list until a large bowl of salad greens appeared under my nose. I looked up to find my grandfather grinning at me.

"Dinner?"

My stomach growled loudly. It felt like a million years had passed since I ate lunch at school. Had that really been just a few hours ago?

Well, a few hours, two polar bears, and a stowaway ago. No wonder I was so hungry.

I put the notebook aside and dug into my salad while my grandfather handed small, rectangular black boxes to everybody else. I looked over with interest as Elliot opened his. I was expecting to see some sort of exotic, dehydrated space food. Like the powdery ice cream I had eaten at the space museum in second grade. But instead, the food inside the box was unmistakably—

"Sushi?" Elliot asked hesitantly.

"Sushi," my grandfather agreed, holding his box at eye level and letting out a deep sigh of satisfaction.

In the next chair over, Venetio was sniffing suspiciously at his box.

"I'm not familiar with sushi," he admitted as he fumbled the lid open. "Is it? I mean, could this really be—"

"Fish," Sylvie finished for him, wrinkling her nose and setting her box (unopened) on the empty seat beside her.

"It's from Sushi Zone," my grandfather informed her, breaking apart his chopsticks with a loud snap so they were ready to use. "The best sushi restaurant in Portland."

"It's still fish," Sylvie said distastefully, pulling a Laffy Taffy rope out of her sweatshirt pocket and unwrapping it.

"Fish," Venetio murmured. He picked up something bright pink perched on top of a mound of rice. "I've heard of fish. Never seen any up close before."

"Never?" Elliot asked through a mouthful of rice. He was already halfway done with his meal. I'd never known Elliot to be particularly keen on sushi. But he was also the least picky eater I had ever met.

"Fish is not very common outside Earth," my grandfather explained, expertly dipping a piece of sushi into a small tub of soy sauce. "I try and stock up on it whenever I'm home. Good barter material. Plus, it's delicious," he added.

He closed his eyes, took a bite, and mmm-hmmed loudly.

Venetio continued to study what I assumed would be his first bite. Eventually.

"It's too cold for liquid water on Pluto," he told us. "No water, no fish."

"Well, at least there's one good thing about Pluto," Sylvie snarked as she bit off an enormous piece of taffy.

Venetio scowled at her, but instead of responding, he took a tiny nibble of his sushi. Nodding with approval, he picked up a glob of green stuff.

"What's this?" he asked, aiming for his mouth.

My grandfather stopped Venetio's hand just in time.

"I wouldn't eat that all at once," he advised and set about explaining to the Plutonian about fiery wasabi and how he could mix it into his soy sauce.

Under the cover of the demonstration, I turned to Sylvie.

"Why don't you like him?" I asked quietly. I was genuinely curious. Sylvie usually liked everybody, unless they did something to annoy her. But she had been snippy with Venetio from the beginning.

Sylvie looked over at me. At some point during the trip, she had removed the clips that usually kept her antennae flat against her head. Her antennae were sticking straight up now. Each of them had a slight kink near the knob on the top, where the clip normally was.

She waved her hand toward Venetio.

"He's a Plutonian," she said impatiently.

I raised an eyebrow.

"And I'm a Martian," she elaborated. "We don't get along."

"You didn't seem to have a problem with Ms. Helen," I pointed out, thinking of how Sylvie had convinced our school's Plutonian administrative assistant to help us break into the school. Twice. Which reminded me of something else...

"Hey, why isn't Ms. Helen blue?"

"She is," Sylvie answered. "She just wears a lot of makeup at school. As to why we get along..." She thought about this for a moment, shredding her Laffy Taffy wrapper as she did. "I guess it's because we don't talk about soccer. Ms. Helen isn't really a fan."

"Soccer?" I asked, thinking about Venetio's ticket. "What, are Martians and Plutonians rivals or something?"

"Sort of," Sylvie grumbled. "I mean, they've never been very good, so it's not much of a rivalry. But they had a decent team in 2014. The 2014 Intergalactic Cup came down to Pluto and Mars, and things got kind of ugly."

"Why?" I asked.

"Because we beat them," Sylvie said immediately. "In the final game of the '14 Finals. One of our best strikers got fouled—"

"'Took a dive,' you mean," Venetio interjected in an icy voice from the other side of the circle. "He dove."

"I said 'fouled,'" Sylvie growled at him. "He got fouled—"

"He took a dive," Venetio said again, gesturing with his chopsticks so violently that the piece of fish he had on the end was in real danger of being flung at Sylvie's head.

"He got fouled," Sylvie insisted.

"Well, I guess you'd know," Venetio said, giving Sylvie a very pointed look.

Sylvie glared at him as Elliot let out a guffaw.

"What would Sylvie know about it?" he scoffed. "She hates sports."

"I was there," Sylvie hissed at him. Then quickly, before Venetio could open his mouth again, she went on. "The score was tied two to two, with just three seconds left in regulation. Tycho Brawn, the best striker in Martian history, got fouled and scored the winning goal off a penalty kick. We—the Martians—won the cup. And the Plutonians have been mad about it ever since."

"Of course we're mad," Venetio said. "You'd be mad too if your team got cheated out of the cup because of a dive—"

"Foul!"

"Dive!"

"Enough!" my grandfather thundered, standing up abruptly.

Sylvie and Venetio were both out of their chairs and glowering at each other across the portal window. My grandfather, who was taller than both of them by at least two feet, scowled at them until they sat back down.

"Word to the wise," my grandfather said, leaning toward me as he settled back into his chair. "Never bring up the '14 Finals in mixed company with Martians and Plutonians. They'll argue about it until they're both blue in the face."

"I'll try and remember that," I said.

I finished my salad and my grandfather took the bowl away, along with an armload of empty sushi boxes. He and Venetio had demolished at least six boxes between them.

Elliot had eaten only one box. Which seemed strange to me. Normally, he ate everything in sight. He had also been sort of quiet today. At the moment, he was stretching out his long legs and glaring at something across the circle.

I followed his eyes. They were fixed on Venetio—who was also staring at him.

"What?" Elliot asked the Plutonian irritably.

"Nothing," Venetio answered. "It's just...you're really tall."

Elliot, who did not enjoy talking about his height, narrowed his eyes even farther at the much-shorter alien.

"Plutonians never get that tall," Venetio continued, sighing wistfully. "We'd give anything to have someone your size on the Kuiper Kickers. Do you play soccer?" he asked, suddenly anxious.

"No," Elliot said, looking like he was trying to decide whether to be annoyed by this conversation or not. "Basketball."

"Are you any good?" Venetio asked.

Elliot looked sort of embarrassed, so I answered for him.

"He's really good," I said. "He even tried out for the county team. They travel all around the state for games and stuff. You have to be really good to play for them."

"Too bad," Venetio said. "With those long arms of yours, you'd make a bang-up goalie."

"Really?" Elliot said thoughtfully. "A goalie?"

"He could never play for you," Sylvie informed Venetio with an odd edge to her voice. "He's an Earthling. Not a Plutonian. He'd never pass the DNA scan."

"Well, there are always ways around that," Venetio muttered.

Sylvie's mouth dropped open, but before she could say anything, there was a loud buzzing sound from her front pocket.

She dug around, eventually extracting her cell phone. When she had it in her hand, she frowned at the screen, hit IGNORE, then shoved the phone back in her pocket.

"You have service?" I asked, incredulous. Shortly after we'd taken off, I'd texted my mom that my grandfather had picked me up early from school for a "surprise research trip" (which I guess was at least technically true), but I hadn't been able to get a signal since.

"I've been on the Martian network since we passed the moon," she said.

"Who was that calling you?" I asked.

"Nobody. Just my mom."

"Oh. Then why didn't you—?"

"I don't want to talk to her right now."

Sylvie bit her lip, and I hesitated, thinking of Mr. Juarez's message.

"You don't want to tell her about the distress signal?" I asked finally.

"We don't even know what it says," Sylvie pointed out. "Not really."

"What do you think he meant?" I asked. "'Tell Sylvie not to'..."

"Worry," Sylvie said immediately. "He was telling her to tell me not to worry. He thinks I worry too much."

"Do you?" I asked.

Sylvie shrugged.

"It looks like I was right to worry this time. Doesn't it?"

Before I could answer, my grandfather came back inside the circle of chairs, grinning and pressing buttons on his iPad.

"We're coming up on Mars!" he told us.

The Problem with Plutonians...

The main thing you notice about Mars when you're really close is that it isn't actually red.

It's more orange. Like tomato soup with a lot of cream in it. There are darker parts too, plus lot of dents and craters. And there's a really big gash that stretches across the middle, kind of like a giant mouth.

We headed straight toward the mouth as we entered Mars orbit and started our descent to the surface. When we got closer, I could see that the gash was actually an enormous canyon with walls so far apart that when we followed one down toward the bottom, we couldn't even see the one on the far side.

Once we were in the canyon, the ground started coming up fast beneath us. And our UFO showed no sign of stopping.

Elliot and I exchanged worried looks across the portal.

"Are we going to crash?" Elliot asked, trying to sound calm.

My grandfather spoke into the iPad instead of answering him.

"Marineris Outpost 6? Marineris Outpost 6? This is the *Lost Beagle*. Come in please."

"Copy, *Lost Beagle*," came a voice from the iPad. "You are cleared to enter Mars. Proceed to the nearest screening dock and have your documentation ready."

The voice was reassuring, but we still weren't slowing down. I braced myself for a crash, suddenly regretting the lack of seat belts. But just before we hit the orangey Martian dirt, the floor of the canyon opened up beneath us and we continued to travel down, past the surface and into the Martian underground.

Across the portal, Elliot's eyes were wide. Mine probably were too. Even though Sylvie had been telling us, pretty much since we found out she was a Martian, that she lived "in Mars" as opposed to "on Mars," the distinction hadn't really hit me until then.

I looked over at my grandfather.

"Are we going to have to wear space suits?" I asked. The thought of squeezing my dinosaur butt into one made me cringe.

He shook his head.

"The underground Martian atmosphere is very similar to Earth. It's a simulation of what Mars's atmosphere used to be like. Before the Martians destroyed it."

"They destroyed their atmosphere?" Elliot asked. "How?"

"The same way humans are currently destroying Earth's," my grandfather said matter-of-factly. "The Martians had to go underground centuries ago to avoid the surface radiation and declining oxygen levels. But don't worry, their underground environment is very suitable for Earth dwellers."

"What about Plutonians?" I asked, looking at Venetio.

"Oh, I'll be cool," Venetio assured me, patting the chest of his black bodysuit. He had zipped it back up over his Kuiper Kickers jersey. "Literally. This is a cold suit. As long as I have it on, I'll be fine. And I don't need nearly as much oxygen as Martians or Earthlings."

"Here," my grandfather said, handing us each something that looked like the gel inserts my dad puts in his tennis shoes. Except these had "Amalgam Labs" written on them instead of "Dr. Scholl's." "Put these inside your shoes. They'll account for the gravitational difference. Mars's gravity is just a little more than one-third of Earth's. Without these, you'd bounce all over the place."

"Awesome!" Elliot grinned. He was taking off his shoes, just like the rest of us, but I could tell from the look on his face that he'd find a way to take the inserts out at the earliest opportunity. "Let's go to Mars!"

"Easy, tiger," my grandfather said. "We have to get through customs first."

◈◈◈

"Craft is named the *Lost Beagle*, registered to Amalgam Labs LLC. Model 2012, Martian engineered, Hohmann class—"

"Actually, it's a 2004," my grandfather corrected the Martian customs official. "Amalgam Labs has done a lot of updating."

The official glanced up at my grandfather. He was short, with extremely round eyes and two pink antennae sticking out of his bald head. He patted the wood-paneled wall beside him with new appreciation.

"A 2004. Never would have guessed," he muttered and then

returned to his form, checking things off as he listed them. "Cargo includes spare parts, miscellaneous lab equipment, one ancient Earth revolver...for which I'm assuming you have the proper paperwork?"

My grandfather handed him a faded piece of paper that said "Antiques Permit." The official read it over, handed it back, and then continued down the form. "One box of ammunition for the revolver, some personal items, and fourteen individually packed restaurant portions of sushi. Crew includes two Earthlings, one dinosaur-Earthling hybrid, one Plutonian, and one Martian-Earthling hybrid."

"Correct," my grandfather agreed.

"It's the Plutonian that's going to be the problem," the official said. Then he looked over at Sylvie and his eyes grew wide. "Say! Are you by any chance—"

"What do you mean the Plutonian is going to be a problem?" my grandfather interrupted.

The official continued squinting at Sylvie for a moment and then turned his attention back to the rest of us.

"Plutonian travel is restricted in Mars," he explained.

"The Planetary Equality Treaty provides for free travel between the planets," Venetio piped up. I got the feeling he had practiced saying that, just in case it ever came up. "The law requires you to permit me entry, sir."

"For now," the official sneered. "Last time I checked, Pluto wasn't exactly a planet anymore. The law is in flux. All Plutonians visiting Mars during the summit are required to have a Martian escort."

"A what?" Venetio squealed.

"An escort. A Martian citizen in good standing who vouches for your behavior and pledges to stay within ten meters of you at all times for the duration of your stay."

"What?" Venetio said again.

The official's eyes came to rest on Sylvie again.

"You're the only Martian here," he pointed out, sounding bored. "Are you willing to act as escort for this Plutonian?"

Sylvie looked over at Venetio. A small smile slid across her face.

"Say it," she commanded.

"Say what?" Venetio asked, raising his eyebrows.

"Foul," Sylvie said, her smile broadening. "Say it was a foul."

"I will not!" Venetio balked, looking shocked at the mere idea.

"Foul," Sylvie encouraged him. "Say it, or no escort for you."

Venetio's hands curled themselves into tiny fists.

"Never," the Plutonian said, shaking with anger.

"Do you want to see that game or not?" Sylvie teased, looking like she was thoroughly enjoying herself. "Say it."

"That's enough, Sylvie," my grandfather finally cut in. "We don't have time for this. If you won't agree to be his escort, we'll have to take him home to Pluto. That will take us at least four days. I don't want to keep your father waiting that long. But it's up to you."

Sylvie scowled, and it was Venetio's turn to grin.

"Fine," she said. "I'll be his stupid escort. Whatever."

The Martian official nodded and slapped matching metal bracelets on Sylvie's and Venetio's wrists.

"If you go farther than ten meters from your escort, an alarm will go off at Central Police Headquarters," the official warned Venetio.

"If it continues to go off for more than thirty seconds, an officer will be dispatched to deport you. There are no second chances. Got it?"

"Got it," Venetio said. Then when the official turned away to go over another form with my grandfather, he muttered, "Way to make a guy feel welcome."

"You're just lucky to be here, Plutonian." Sylvie sniffed.

"Geez, Sylvie. Why do you have to be so mean to him?" Elliot asked her.

Sylvie rolled her eyes and ignored him.

Privately, I agreed with Elliot. Venetio seemed OK. And aside from the fact that their planets' soccer teams were rivals, I really didn't see what Sylvie's problem was.

◆◆◆

The Martian official went belowdecks after that. To check that we weren't hiding any BURPSers in the lower decks, I guess. My grandfather gathered us all together.

"As far as the Martian authorities are concerned, we're here to refuel," my grandfather informed us. "That usually wouldn't take us more than a couple of hours, but I fooled around with the turborotor and a few other things. Enough so we'll have to stay here for a few days to make repairs. Hopefully, that will give us enough time to locate Sylvie's dad."

"How are we going to do that?" Sylvie asked. "Can you trace the source of that transmission you found? Or find the lab some other way?"

"I have it covered," my grandfather assured her with a wink. "But first, we need to talk about Mars. There's a lot going on here, what with the summit and the game and everything. I don't want us to get involved in any of that. Those things have nothing to do with us. Our goal is to find Sylvie's father. The key to accomplishing that is for us all to keep a low profile. If we keep our heads down and don't draw any attention to ourselves, everything will be fine. OK?"

Elliot, Sylvie, and I nodded.

"Er…" Venetio stammered, looking embarrassed.

"What?" my grandfather demanded.

"Nothing!" Venetio assured him, shoving what looked like a phone into the front pocket of his suit.

My grandfather gave him a suspicious look, but he was prevented from pursuing the matter further by the reappearance of the Martian official.

"It all looks legal, though I'd say you have some rotor damage," he remarked.

"I was afraid of that," my grandfather said gravely. "Can you point us in the direction of a good repair shop?"

"Sure thing," the official said, turning to open the portal door and usher us all off the ship. "What the—"

There was a sea of faces waiting for us outside. Small, pinkish faces with perfectly round eyes, tiny mouths, and flat ears. And antennae. Everyone in sight had two bobbing antennae sticking out of the top of their heads.

I barely had time to notice that most of the Martians had bushy hair like Sylvie before there was a great roar of excitement, followed by a blinding series of flashbulbs.

For a horrible moment, I thought that the crowd and all the hubbub were about me. I felt every bit as self-conscious as I had on the first day of fifth grade, the first time I had had to face all of my classmates as a half-dinosaur. And a huge part of my brain started trying to figure out how I could melt myself right down into the floor.

But then I heard what the voices were saying:

"SYL-VI-A!" they chanted. "SYL-VI-A! SYL-VI-A!"

Twenty-Two

The five of us, plus the Customs official, stood stunned in the doorway of the ship for some time before a swarm of Martians wearing black helmets and riot gear hustled us away. I grasped the end of my tail tightly to keep it from getting stepped on as we were hurried along. Shouts of "SYL-VI-A!" and "TWENTY-TWO! TWENTY-TWO!" followed us down a hallway until we were shoved unceremoniously into a small room. Which, from the smell of things, was used to hold cleaning supplies.

Our guards shut the door behind them and left us there. We stood blinking in the dim light, trying to clear the residual echo of the flashbulbs out of our eyes.

Once we could see again, we all stared at Sylvie.

She was examining her right thumbnail, carefully not looking at any of us.

I cleared my throat.

"Um, any chance you're going to tell us what that was all about?"

Sylvie narrowed her eyes at her thumb.

"What *what* was all about?" she asked innocently.

"Sylvie!" I exclaimed.

"OK, OK." She stared harder at her thumb and then took a big deep breath.

"I guess you could say…" she started. "I mean, you wouldn't be totally wrong if you thought… I guess I'm a little bit…famous."

"Famous?" Elliot echoed her.

"Kinda," she said quietly.

"Wait, you guys don't know?" Venetio piped in. And for the first time, I glared at him. I wasn't sure I liked this Plutonian knowing something about my friend that I didn't.

"What's 'twenty-two'?" my grandfather asked with raised eyebrows.

"That was my jersey number," she told him.

"Jersey?" I asked, and then it all came together in my head at once. "Soccer! It was you, wasn't it?"

Sylvie just stared at me.

"In the '14 Finals," I explained. "You were the one who took a dive—er, I mean—got fouled. Weren't you?"

"Sylvie? Play soccer?" Elliot asked, laughing. "No way. I don't believe it."

I understood his skepticism. The Sylvie we knew hated sports. And exercise. And sunlight. But that was the only thing I could think of that made sense.

Sylvie let out a deep sigh.

"OK, fine. I was on the team. And I did play in the '14 Finals. But I wasn't the one who got fouled."

"She wasn't," Venetio cut in. "It was Tycho Brawn who took the dive."

"But you played soccer?" Elliot exclaimed, still stuck on what he plainly considered to be the most important detail.

"Yes," Sylvie said simply. "I played soccer. And I was awesome, OK? But I don't play anymore."

I felt like my brain was doing somersaults inside my skull. Even before we had found out she was a Martian (well, half-Martian), Elliot and I had always known that Sylvie was a bit…odd. And that she probably had secrets. But this…

"Why didn't you tell us?" I demanded.

She shrugged. "You never asked."

"That's not something you wait to be asked!" I exclaimed, suddenly really frustrated. "Friends are supposed to tell their other friends important stuff like this!"

"Well, I didn't know that rule until now." Sylvie sniffed and looked sulkily at the floor.

Venetio turned to my grandfather.

"You didn't know who she was either, sir?" he asked incredulously.

"Please stop calling me 'sir.' And I don't follow soccer," my grandfather said. Then he turned back to Sylvie. "I do wish you had said something, young lady. I'm afraid this is going to complicate the incognito plan."

"Sorry," said Sylvie, not sounding sorry at all. "But nobody would have even known I was back if not for the big-mouthed Plutonian over there."

Everyone's gaze shifted over to Venetio, who raised his hands defensively.

"Admit it," Sylvie said angrily. "You told."

She fixed the Plutonian with a look that I had seen her mother use on uncooperative restaurant staff. It had the same effect on Venetio that it had had on the servers. He began to squirm uncomfortably and looked appealingly at my grandfather.

"I only told my mom! I called her, sir, just like you told me to. She's a big soccer fan. I had to tell her I'd gotten a ride to Mars with Sylvia Juarez!"

"Your mother was your only call?" my grandfather growled.

"Um, well, yes, sir. But I have a feeling she may have called a few more people. Like, maybe the radio station that gave me the ticket."

"I have a feeling you're right," my grandfather said, letting out a deep sigh.

The Martian police eventually returned to let us out. By then, we had all decided that we should spend the night at Sylvie's apartment. It was nearby and conveniently empty, since Sylvie's mom was on Earth and Sylvie's dad was still missing.

By the time we got there, I was so tired I could barely keep my eyes open. But since this was my first time in a Martian apartment, I managed to notice (and be disappointed by) the fact that it looked pretty much like a regular Earth apartment. Sort of. Except that almost everything was made out of metal. The walls, the furniture, and even the floors were all gleaming and metallic. Between those and the large windows, which looked out over another apartment building next door, the place felt a little bit like a giant aquarium.

I went to sleep that night in camel position. But even so, I felt a bit like a hamster. Or a maybe a lizard. Or some other animal that lived in a glass cage…

◆◆◆

The next morning, sunlight was streaming through the humongous floor-to-ceiling windows in my room.

My brain registered that as odd, since we were underground, but then my stomach called attention to itself with a warning growl. My dinosaur appetite was not something to be trifled with, and I had eaten rather lightly yesterday. Today, it seemed, my stomach was taking action to make sure that didn't happen again.

On the other side of the bed, Elliot was still asleep. Flat on his back, with one arm thrown over his eyes. His feet were hanging so far off the end of the tiny, Martian-sized mattress that he looked like one of those melted clocks in the Salvador Dalí paintings we had studied in art.

I tiptoed out of the room so as not to wake him.

Across the hall, the door to Sylvie's room was shut. She must still be asleep too. The heap of blankets outside her door (Venetio's bed, since there was no actual bed within ten meters of Sylvie's) was empty. The Plutonian at least was awake.

I found him sitting awkwardly in the middle of the kitchen.

The Juarezes' kitchen was one of those weird, fancy, ginormous kitchens where it's hard to find the refrigerator. I guess the fanciness made sense, considering that both of Sylvie's parents were trained chefs. There were several rows of cabinets without any obvious way to open them and two large islands. There was also a very serious-looking stove, which my grandfather was standing in front of. He raised a spatula to me in greeting and then continued muttering to himself as he banged around several skillets.

I looked back down at Venetio. He had a plateful of eggs balanced on his lap. I gestured to the empty kitchen table on the other side of the room.

"Why—" I began.

He raised one arm in the air—the one with the tracking bracelet the Martian customs official had put on him yesterday. Then he very deliberately moved his wrist an inch farther from the door.

The bracelet emitted a high-pitched beeping sound, which made me jump. Venetio pulled his arm back and the beeping stopped.

"This is as far from her as I'm allowed to go," he explained. Then, raising his voice and angling his head so that his words rumbled down the hallway, "So I'll just sit on the *floor*! Until *somebody* decides to get her lazy, Martian butt out of bed!"

"Bite me, Pluto!" came an enraged voice from down the hall behind Sylvie's door. "I'm getting my beauty rest here!"

"Good luck with that!" Venetio sneered. He shoveled a forkful of eggs into his mouth and turned his attention back to the enormous flat screen on the wall. On TV, a Martian with an enormous amount of gel in his hair was grinning broadly from behind a desk.

"Welcome to MBC-E, the Martian Broadcast Company's English-language affiliate! Mars's only all-English, all-the-time channel! In a moment, we'll continue with our *Big Bang Theory* marathon, catching you up just in time for the big finale later this week. But first, the news."

"Ohhh!" Venetio enthused, pumping a fist and nearly dumping his eggs onto the floor. "I love that show! We get it on Pluto too. Do you think they get *Dancing with the Stars* here? We're like three seasons behind on that one."

"They get it," my grandfather informed him. "It came on right after *American Idol* this morning."

"Weird," I muttered, trying not to step on Venetio as I went to take a seat at the empty table. "Just weird."

"With two days until the summit, security is at an all-time high here in Mars Central," continued the Martian newscaster as a picture of a rotund, half-bald Martian appeared on the screen, "Chancellor Gio has assured all of us here at MBC-E that every safety precaution is being taken."

"Chancellor Gio…is that the Martian leader?" I asked.

"Actually, Mars is run by an elected council," my grandfather answered from behind the stove. "But they appoint chancellors to be in charge of certain areas, as well as special events. Chancellor Gio is the one in charge of the summit. Omelet?"

"Er, OK," I said politely. My stomach had started growling again. Even though it didn't really want an omelet.

"I know eggs aren't usually on the herbivore menu," my grandfather said apologetically. "Greens are pretty scarce in Mars. Hard to grow them here, you know? But I did find some mushrooms in the freezer," he said, tipping one of the pans in my direction so I could see a pile of button mushrooms swimming around in butter and garlic. "And there was a box of these on the counter," he added, tossing me something wrapped in plastic.

The package was small, no larger than my palm. But it was surprisingly heavy in my hand. I turned it over so I could see the label.

"Nutri Nugget," I read. "One-third of your daily nutritional needs. Cocoa flavored."

"They're all the rage here," my grandfather informed me.

Inside the package was a soft, brown, vaguely rectangular object that looked disturbingly like—

"A turd," Venetio said through a mouthful of eggs. Swallowing, he nodded confidently to himself. "That's what they look like. Turds. Taste like 'em too."

I set the unopened nugget on the table in front of me.

"Maybe I'll try the eggs."

The Plutonian and I sat in silence, watching Martian TV, while my grandfather poured a bowl full of beaten eggs into the mushroom pan. The newscaster finished the news-news and moved on to entertainment-news. I nearly fell off my chair when a picture of Sylvie, my grandfather, Elliot, Venetio, and I standing on the gangplank of the *Lost Beagle* appeared on-screen.

"On the heels of the announcement that Tycho Brawn will be coming out of retirement to play in the summit's Friendship and Goodwill Game, another famous Martian striker has returned home! That's right, folks! Everybody's favorite big-haired, sharp-tongued Razer is back in planet! Is she here to play? So far, all parties involved are staying tight-lipped. But check out her entourage, why don't you? Two Earthlings, a Plutonian, and a dinosaur-Earthling hybrid! Leave it to Sylvia Juarez to arrive in style!"

My grandfather set a plate down in front of me. It was an omelet dotted with mushrooms and some sort of white cheese. My stomach gave a displeased lurch, but my tail twitched automatically at the scent of food.

I motioned to the chair next to me, but my grandfather shook his head and set his plate on the closest kitchen island.

"I'll stand, thanks," he said and leaned against the countertop.

I picked up my fork and tried to look excited. But as I glanced back and forth between the plate of eggy, cheesy fungus and the partially unwrapped turd, I could think of only one thing: I would have given anything for a nice, crisp salad.

To cover up the fact that I wasn't eating, I motioned to the other kitchen island. My grandfather had set up a temporary laboratory there. Complete with test tubes, a Bunsen burner, and a couple of gadgety things with wires sticking out in all directions.

"What's all that?" I asked.

"That is how we're going to find Sylvie's dad and Sunder Labs," my grandfather answered, spearing three mushrooms onto his fork at once. "The things with the wires are devices that track people based on their DNA signature. In theory anyway."

"Do you know how they work?" I asked, picking up my fork and poking cautiously at my omelet.

"I should hope so. I invented them!" he snorted, with a note of pride in his voice. "Actually, they're still in the beta-testing phase. Only the short-range one is working at the moment. I'm hoping to get the long-range scanner working by this afternoon."

"What do we do until then?" I asked, still picking through the omelet with my fork, delaying the inevitable first bite.

"Oh, I should think you'll be busy enough today. If I know the Martians, and I think I do, I'd say it's about to get very crowded in here. How's the omelet?"

Unable to avoid it any longer, I took a bite. I had intended to swallow it quickly and then tell my grandfather it was "great." But my body absolutely refused to comply with this request. I ended up spitting the whole mouthful right back onto my plate. Eggs had never been my favorite. And these tasted like no eggs I had ever had before.

"What is this?" I heard myself ask, as Venetio snorted with laughter from the floor.

"Oh, you mean the Bruno eggs?"

"The what?"

"Brunos," my grandfather explained patiently, "are a species of lizard native to the underground caves of Mars. What? You didn't think there'd be chicken eggs here, did you?"

Razer No More

My grandfather was right. By the time I had eaten the Nutri Nugget (which, to my relief, tasted more like chocolate than Venetio had led me to believe) and woken up Elliot and Sylvie, there were ten Martians in the living room.

They were all surrounding one lone, blue figure. At first, I thought it was Venetio. But then I saw him lurking unhappily in the far corner of the room.

The other blue figure raised its hand and gave me a small, almost shy wave.

"Ms. Helen!" Elliot and I both exclaimed at once.

"Oh, that's right!" my grandfather exclaimed. "I forgot you guys already know Helen Tombaugh."

"Hello, Sawyer," she said, shaking my hand warmly. I smiled in return, trying to cover up my shock at seeing her without makeup. She was as blue as Venetio. And she was *here*. I was used to seeing

Ms. Helen sitting, more or less permanently, behind her desk in the frigidly cold front office of our school. She always wore sleeveless shirts and had a large fan blowing directly in her face. But now she was standing upright. And wearing a black bodysuit like Venetio's.

"What are you doing here?" Sylvie asked her suspiciously.

"I'm here for the summit," Ms. Helen answered. "I took a leave of absence from my office job at your school in order to represent Pluto. May I introduce Chancellor Fontana, my Martian escort?"

A Martian woman with hair that was curly and poufy like Sylvie's, but extremely blond, stuck her pinkish hand out for me to shake.

"Pleasure to meet you, Sawyer," she said. "I'm Claire Fontana, temporary Chancellor in Charge of Martian-Human Affairs."

"Temporary?" I asked, wondering why the title sounded so familiar.

When I remembered, I swallowed hastily. That was Sylvie's dad's job. This woman must be filling in for him.

"Oh," I said, looking down at the floor.

The other Martians were all chancellors in charge of this or that. They all introduced themselves except for one particularly short and bald Martian who hung back. He waited until everyone else was done talking, then stepped forward and smiled at Sylvie.

"Coach Kepler," Sylvie said, not smiling in return.

"Hello, Sylvia," the coach said, and only then did I realize that his bright-red jacket had *Razers* written down both sleeves. "I'm here to formally offer you a place on the Red Razers."

He reached into one of the pockets in his jacket and pulled out a red piece of cloth. With a showy flourish, he shook it out so that we could see that it was a red soccer jersey.

It had *Juarez* and *22* written on it in glittery, silver letters.

The Martians standing around us, including Chancellor Fontana, all burst into applause.

"Thank you," Sylvie said tonelessly over the din. "But I decline."

"What?" Elliot exclaimed.

"What?" the coach exclaimed, sounding more angry than shocked.

"I'm retired," Sylvie explained.

"I told you," Ms. Helen mumbled, a ghost of a smile on her lips.

"Ms. Juarez…" the coach began, and the hand holding the red jersey dropped to his side like a flag at half-mast. "Sylvia. This is a key moment for the Razers. A seminal moment in the history of intergalactic sports! Your planet needs you. I beg you to reconsider."

"Sorry," Sylvie said. Her face was carefully expressionless, but I could see her fingers angrily twisting the sleeves of her oversized sweatshirt. "I'm not here to play. I'm here to visit my father. Have you seen him?"

The coach took a step back and exchanged a look with the Martian standing nearest to him. Suddenly, nobody in the room seemed able to look Sylvie in the eye.

"Uh, no, as a matter of fact I haven't seen him. Not recently," the coach said finally, addressing the lamp several feet to Sylvie's left.

"Well then, I suggest you come back when you have," Sylvie said. "You want me to play? Then find my father. Until you do that, I have nothing further to say to you. Understand?"

The Martians and Ms. Helen retreated to one corner of the living room to talk among themselves. My grandfather pulled Sylvie and me out of earshot.

"Sylvie," he said sternly, "I realize that Venetio blew the initial plan by telling everyone you had returned to Mars. But we still intended to stay under the radar and search for your father quietly. What you've just done—"

"What I've just done," Sylvie retorted, "is get an entire planet looking for my father. If they want me to play, they'll find him. Now, if anybody needs me, I'll be in my room."

She turned on her heel to stomp away, but my grandfather caught her arm before she could take a step.

"Oh, no you don't. Chancellor Fontana and Ms. Helen have set up a tour for you guys, and you're all going."

"A tour?" I asked, ears perking. "Of Mars?"

"Not all of Mars, just the downtown area around the apartment. But it'll be a perfect opportunity for you to take the short-range scanner out of the apartment and see if Sylvie's dad is nearby."

As he spoke, he slapped the scanner onto my wrist like a watch and pulled my long-sleeved T-shirt down to hide it.

Sylvie held up a finger.

"Number one, I highly doubt a secret laboratory is hidden somewhere downtown. Number two," she continued, throwing up another finger, "I was born here. I don't need a tour."

My grandfather held up two fingers of his own.

"Number one, if you're right about the lab not being downtown, then we're going to need the long-range scanner to find it. Which

74

is currently broken. And, number two, I can't fix it with all of these people hanging around the apartment. So be a good little celebrity, go on your tour, and leave me in peace."

Sylvie rolled her eyes and then walked dramatically toward the front door.

"I'll be waiting in the hallway," she announced loudly for the benefit of the crowd on the other side of the living room. "I'm so excited about the tour!"

The door slammed behind her.

A few seconds later, Venetio bolted out after her, his wrist monitor beeping like mad.

Mars Central

Coach Kepler and most of the other Martians begged off, so the tour ended up consisting of me, Elliot, Sylvie, Venetio, Ms. Helen, Chancellor Fontana, and a few Martian police officers in black outfits and face shields.

"I gave tours for a living before I got the chancellor job," Chancellor Fontana chirped excitedly, as we rode the elevator down to street level. "I can tell you everything you'd like to know about our charming planet!"

"How long have you been a chancellor?" I asked her. I suspected it couldn't be long, since she had taken over Mr. Juarez's job.

It wasn't.

"Two weeks," she said cheerfully.

I peeked down at the scanner, trying to make it look like I was just checking a really oversized watch. The screen had the outline of a map on it, kind of like GPS. My grandfather had explained that if the scanner picked up Mr. Juarez's DNA signature, it would appear on the map as a red dot. There should also be a beeping sound.

Nothing so far.

I covered up the scanner again, just as the elevator dinged and we all followed Chancellor Fontana through the lobby and out onto the streets of Mars.

When Sylvie had first told me that Martians live beneath the surface, I had pictured a world where herds of tiny Martians wandered around a dark network of caves and tunnels. There was dirt. Lots of dirt. Everyone was sort of grubby and mole-like, blinking at each other in the dim, faintly red light.

The actual Martian world was pretty much the opposite of that.

First of all, it was light. Really light. Everything around us was made out of metal or glass, just like Sylvie's apartment building. And it was all extremely clean, like someone had just come along and given everything in sight a good scrubbing. So my first impression of Mars was that it was quite shiny.

It was easy to forget that we were underground. The caverns that made up Mars Central (which most people just seemed to call "Central") were big enough that the buildings around us were as tall as any skyscrapers you'd see in an Earth city. It was only when you looked straight up that you could tell there was actually a metal roof up there with a simulated sky projected onto it.

"Central is roughly the size of New York City on Earth," said

Chancellor Fontana, facing us and walking backward as she talked with the effortlessness of a trained tour guide. "We have a similar population density and many of the same challenges that come with so many people living in such close proximity."

Her words made my heart sink. It had been hard enough to picture finding Sylvie's dad in a maze of dark, underground caves. But how were we possibly going to find him in a city the size of New York?

I snuck another peek at the scanner: no red dot yet.

Chancellor Fontana went on to discuss the light. It was artificially created and in perfect synch with the light on the planet's surface. So when the sun went down on the surface, the light beneath the surface dimmed as well. Which explained how I had seen the sunrise from Sylvie's guest room that morning. There was even manufactured moonlight that corresponded to the phases of Mars's two moons, Phobos and Deimos.

"No stars though," Sylvie told us. "You have to go to one of the observatories if you want to see stars."

The streets were crowded with pedestrians. Most of the people we passed were Martians, of course. But I also noticed a fair number of blue-skinned Plutonians, all sticking close to their Martian escorts. There were a few tall, thin Jupiterians and a smattering of other folks who I couldn't immediately place. They must have been from other planets. Some were in tight-fitting space suits like Venetio and Ms. Helen. But most people wore loose, flowy things, like robes or roomy pants.

A lot of the people around us recognized Sylvie. Chancellor Fontana kept us going at a brisk pace, and stern looks from the Martian police officers kept people from getting too close. But there were lots of cries of "Sylvia!" and "Fear the Red!" I thought I heard a few yells of "Dinosaur Kid!" and "Hey, Dino Boy!" but I couldn't be sure.

Sylvie cringed at each new voice and tugged the hood of her sweatshirt down over her eyes.

"If you really want to hide, you might want to think about getting a different-colored sweatshirt," Elliot said helpfully.

Sylvie only glared at him.

"Central is the most diverse city in the galaxy," Chancellor Fontana bragged, as a gaggle of girl Martians—all wearing red, number 22, Red Razer jerseys—pointed at Sylvie and squealed. "We are truly an intergalactic city with a population representing all eight planets."

"Nine," I heard Venetio mutter under his breath. "All nine planets."

"Even Earth?" Elliot inquired.

Our guide paused, looking a tad embarrassed.

"Well, we're still working on that one. Earthlings don't officially know of our existence yet, of course. But everyone is welcome in Central!"

"Except Plutonians," Venetio growled under his breath, looking down at his tracking bracelet.

The streets and sidewalks were all made of metal. The hard surface felt weird under my feet, kind of like I was walking up the front of a stainless-steel refrigerator. It was smooth enough that it didn't scrape against the bottom of my tail when I walked, which was nice. But the hard surface made my tennis balls bounce in all directions, so I ended up holding the end of my tail in my hand. I couldn't afford to lose any tennis balls here. Finding a replacement might be tricky—I didn't know if Martians even played tennis.

We arrived at a large intersection where several streets came together at once. Chancellor Fontana stopped us just underneath an enormous digital screen and started saying something about the architecture of one of the buildings nearby.

"…and the turrets are rather obviously based on the famous Trident Hall on Neptune. While the distinctive fluted columns around the entrance give the building more of a late-Venutian-Renaissance, second-period Mercurian influence…"

I tuned her out and watched as a spiky-haired Martian in a black police uniform spoke solemnly from the depths of the large screen, first in Martian, then in English:

The security threat level in Mars Central remains high. All Martian citizens and summit visitors are urged to keep a sharp eye out for BURPSers and to report any suspicious activity to Martian officials immediately.

The announcement caused several Martians and at least one Jupiterian nearby to look suspiciously at Venetio.

"He's not a BURPSer," Elliot informed them angrily. "He's just a Plutonian."

"They don't care," Venetio said quietly to Elliot. "Some people just hate all Plutonians. BURPSers or not. They think we're troublemakers."

"Has it ever occurred to you," Sylvie said to him, "that if your planet stopped causing so much trouble, people would be nicer to you?"

Venetio shrugged.

"Maybe if people were nicer to us, we'd stop causing so much trouble."

Sylvie looked like she was about to respond, but she cut herself off when a new picture appeared on the screen.

It was a short, nondescript Martian with glasses and a bad comb-over. Just a few inches to my right, Sylvie went rigid. When the English headline popped up underneath the Martian's face, I understood why.

> MISSING: Asaph Juarez, former Chancellor in Charge of Martian–Human Affairs. Please contact the Martian Council with any relevant information.

"That's a good thing, isn't it?" I said uneasily, patting Sylvie on the shoulder. "The more people who are looking for him, the better. Right?"

Sylvie swallowed.

"I guess so. I just…I was hoping it was all some sort of misunderstanding. That I'd get here and he'd be sitting in our kitchen with no idea anything was going on. But if the Martian Council doesn't know where he is, that means he really is missing."

"We'll find him," I assured her. We both looked down at my wrist, even though neither of us had heard a beep. No dot yet.

"You were probably right about the lab not being downtown," I told her. "Once my grandfather gets the long-range scanner up and running, we'll find your dad."

Sylvie nodded and a shrill beeping sound filled the air. We looked around in confusion, and it took me almost a full minute to realize that every watch on every Martian in sight had just started beeping.

Every watch except mine.

The Debate

"**N**ug time!" exclaimed Chancellor Fontana, quieting her watch and pulling a Nutri Nugget out of her purse.

Every Martian around us (except for Sylvie) was doing the same thing. There was a great crinkling of plastic as everyone opened their nuggets at once.

Sylvie wrinkled her nose.

"I can't believe those got popular," she sniffed. "They're disgusting!"

"You're right about that," Venetio muttered. Then he pursed his lips, looking mildly horrified that he had agreed with Sylvie about something.

"The one I had this morning wasn't too bad," I admitted. And I realized, to my amazement, that my stomach had been quiet for some time. I hadn't even thought about food since shoving the nugget into my mouth that morning. Now that I did think about it, I realized that I still felt full. But in a weird, hollow sort of a way. Like I could still eat a giant meal at any moment but I just didn't want to.

"I have extras," Chancellor Fontana offered, reaching into her purse again and handing me several different flavors. There was a chocolate-flavored nugget like the one I had eaten that morning. There was also a strawberry-flavored one, a root beer–flavored one, and a chocolate-peanut-butter-swirl one.

"What are they?" Elliot asked, looking doubtfully at the packages in my hand. He had slept too late that morning to hear anything about the nuggets.

"They're a revelation," Chancellor Fontana replied, licking her fingers. "Do you have any idea how much time and energy is wasted in the growing of food? To say nothing of harvesting, preparing, and then consuming elaborate meals three times every day?"

"Of course they don't," Ms. Helen reminded her, taking a bite of her own nugget. "Plants and animals grow by accident on their planet, remember?"

"Oh right," Chancellor Fontana said. "Well, just take my word for it. You'd be amazed at how freeing it is to not have to worry about preparing food. I don't know how we ever got along without these things! They've quite revolutionized Martian culture."

Despite Chancellor Fontana's enthusiasm, Elliot was looking doubtfully at the brown rectangle in his hand.

"It kind of reminds me of something," he said, turning it around in his hands. "I'm trying to think of what…"

"If you don't like the texture, then I have just the thing,"

Chancellor Fontana said, reaching into her purse again and handing Elliot a small bottle.

"Nutri Juice," Elliot read.

"The next generation of condensed nutrition. Same thing as the nuggets, but in liquid form!" Chancellor Fontana explained, taking a quick glance around us. "Don't let on that I gave you that. They're not on the market yet. The plan is to reveal them for the first time during the toast after the Friendship and Goodwill Game."

"The toast?" I asked.

"There's a toast at the end of every Intergalactic Soccer Federation game," Venetio told us. "The winners pour the losers a drink, and the losers have to toast the winners while they take a sip. It's about sportsmanship and stuff. The drink is supposed to be something special and meaningful from the winner's home planet."

"But," Sylvie cut in, "since the losers have to drink it and the winners don't, it usually ends up being the most disgusting drink the winning team can think of."

"Really?" I asked.

Sylvie nodded solemnly.

"Oh yeah. After we won the '14 Finals, we poured the Plutonians raw Bruno egg whites. Some of them actually threw up on camera."

"Nutri Juice isn't too bad," Ms. Helen admitted. "I think the Plutonians will get off easy this time."

Everyone looked expectantly at Elliot.

Elliot grinned sheepishly and handed me the Nutri Juice.

"Maybe I'm not quite as hungry as I thought."

We eventually made it out toward the outskirts of the city. We started walking through caverns that weren't quite as tall with walls that weren't quite as smooth. In some places, the walls were covered in thin wire mesh and I could see orangey-red Martian dirt peeking through.

"Central is constantly expanding," Chancellor Fontana droned on. "Our population rises at a steady rate each year, and engineers work around the clock to create more livable areas."

We passed a wall that had three large, gaping holes in it. I couldn't see too far inside any of them, but I could hear the hum of working machinery. There was also a touch of reddish dust in the air.

Elliot sneezed loudly.

"What's that?" Sylvie asked, pointing at a fourth hole. It was smaller than the others, and it had strips of red tape crisscrossing its entrance.

"Oh, the engineers must have hit a vein of iron ore," our guide explained. "Or possibly peridotite. Those are the densest kinds of rocks on Mars. They're great if you're looking to mine them, but they're not really cost effective to dig through. We tunnel around them when we can."

"You mean you can't get through them?" Sylvie asked.

"We can," Chancellor Fontana replied, sounding a bit miffed at the suggestion that they couldn't. "But it takes longer and it costs more. Not really worth doing when so much of Mars is made up of sediments and siltstone."

"Huh," Sylvie said thoughtfully, as our guide steered us away from the tunnels and back toward the larger caverns of downtown Central.

◆◆◆

As we walked back toward Sylvie's apartment, we passed the big screen again. A large crowd was gathered underneath it now, and a tight circle of Martian police ringed a temporary stage.

Three people were on the stage. One was a red-faced Martian who was yelling and shaking his fist at a Plutonian with a spiky black Mohawk. Between them was the nearly bald Martian who I recognized from TV as Chancellor Gio, the Martian in charge of the summit.

"Thank you. Now if we could just hear from the opposing side—" Chancellor Gio was saying, trying to get a word in edgewise as the Martian continued to gesture violently at his blue counterpart on the other side of the stage.

"It's simple! The Interplanetary Soccer Federation is an organization for planets. And Pluto is no longer a planet. That's why I am urging the Martian Council to vote YES on the measure to ban Pluto from the ISF."

There was a roar of approval from the crowd, even as the Plutonian shook his head vigorously.

"Pluto *is* a planet," he argued. "We're a dwarf planet. That's still a planet. And besides, the ISF is the only league of its kind in the galaxy. Our team would have nowhere to play! Soccer is our biggest export. It's essential to our planetary identity!"

"Then why don't you start a dwarf planet soccer league?" the

Martian suggested. "One that would be better suited for an orbiting body of your size and limited gravitational pull!"

The crowd roared with laughter, and I leaned over toward Ms. Helen.

"They're trying to ban Plutonians from the soccer federation?" I asked.

She nodded grimly.

"That's what the summit is all about," she said. She had to practically shout to be heard over the crowd. "The vote is in two days, right after the Friendship and Goodwill Game. If it passes, Pluto will be permanently banned. The Kuiper Kickers will be disbanded."

I looked worriedly over at Venetio. His eyes were locked on the sweaty Martian onstage. His hands had curled up into small, blue fists at his sides.

"That seems really unfair," I said.

The Plutonian onstage seemed to agree.

"First, you downgrade our planetary status," he accused the Martian. "Now you want to kick us out of the ISF. What's next? When will it end? Your prejudice against Pluto is baseless and—"

"This isn't about prejudice!" the Martian exclaimed. "This is about safety! Where the Kuiper Kickers go, the BURPSers follow. ISF fans have a right to be safe. No one should have to risk their lives in order to enjoy a soccer game! Booting the Plutonians will make the games safer. We haven't forgotten what you tried to do on Neptune—"

"What the *BURPSers* tried to do on Neptune," the Plutonian corrected him angrily. "As I've said before, the BURPSers do not represent the interests of the majority of the gentle, peace-loving people of Pluto who—"

"The 'gentle' and 'peace-loving' thugs who tried to blow up the planetary core of their nearest neighbor?" the Martian demanded.

"Thank you both for expressing your views!" Chancellor Gio jumped in, trying to put himself between the two debaters. "Now, I'd like to move on to the question-and-answer portion of the—"

"That is a ridiculous overstatement of the facts," the Plutonian debater shouted over Chancellor Gio's head. "The BURPSers do not have anywhere near the capacity to blow up an entire planet—"

"And how would you know that," the Martian countered, a giant grin spilling over his face, "unless you were a BURPSer *yourself*!"

The crowd gasped, and the Plutonian looked affronted.

"I'm an adopted Martian citizen! I was born and raised here!"

"BURPSer!" the Martian yelled, pointing. "BURPSer!"

The crowd took up the chant.

"BURPSer! BURPSer!"

"This is insanity," Ms. Helen muttered, pulling me backward and out of the path of several black-clad Martian police officers who were headed toward the stage.

The Plutonian onstage was still loudly denying the Martian debater's allegations, but it was impossible to hear him over the yelling of the crowd. Chancellor Gio was waving his arms frantically.

"Quiet!" he ordered. "Quiet! If we're going to have a meaningful debate—"

The yelling basically drowned the chancellor out. But he kept talking. I couldn't understand his words anymore, but we all heard the groan of pain that came out of his lips next.

The crowd fell silent as Chancellor Gio sank to his knees. A larger-than-life picture of him appeared on the huge screen. He was clutching the left side of his neck, which had started to swell. There was a lump there, which was pulsing slightly. As though there was something underneath his skin, trying to get out.

The chancellor's groan turned into a strangled yell. Then the skin split beneath his hand and something came out. Something with hair. And a face.

Everyone in the square froze in shock as the chancellor's second head slowly emerged out of its neck. Its eyes blinked fiercely as its mouth opened up in a huge yawn, like it was waking up from a long nap.

Gene-ing

I t's called gene-ing," my grandfather explained after Chancellor Fontana and Ms. Helen managed to extract us from the crowd in the square and returned us to the Juarezes' apartment.

We had found my grandfather exactly where we had left him: in the kitchen, fighting with the long-range DNA scanner.

"Gene-ing?" I asked.

"Infecting someone with a virus that contains foreign genetic material," he explained, jabbing at the scanner with a screwdriver. "Usually there's also some sort of accelerator involved to make the genetic mutation happen faster than it would normally."

"Is it like what happened at Amalgam Labs?" I asked. "Like the virus that turned some of the scientists into dinosaur-human hybrids?"

"Very like," my grandfather admitted. "Only that was an accident. Officially anyway. These ones however…"

"These ones are clearly being done on purpose," Ms. Helen

finished, putting down the untouched cup of coffee my grandfather had poured for her.

"These *ones*?" Elliot and I said together.

Ms. Helen looked over at Chancellor Fontana, who sighed.

"Chancellor Gio was the third Chancellor to get gened in the last week," she admitted. "Now the committee will have to elect a new chancellor and hope he or she can avoid being gened for long enough to get through the summit."

"Who will they elect?" Elliot asked.

"I'm not sure," Ms. Helen admitted. "But it's getting harder to find volunteers."

When everybody else made their way to the living room, I stayed behind with my grandfather.

"Did you know the summit was about kicking the Plutonians out of the Intergalactic Soccer Federation?" I asked him.

My grandfather scratched an itchy spot on the back of his neck and stretched, grunting.

"That's what I meant when I told you about the local politics. It's not something you need to worry about, Sawyer."

"But doesn't it seem unfair to you? Why should the Martians be able to decide if the Plutonians get to play soccer or not? Aren't there other planets in the federation?"

"Yes, but control of the ISF rotates among its members. This year, Mars is in charge. Which means they get to speak for everybody. The Martian Council gets to have the final word at the summit."

"It sounds to me like they've just been waiting for their year to get rid of their biggest rival," I muttered.

My grandfather nodded. "You might be right. It probably is unfair, Sawyer. But who are we to say anything about it? It's nothing to do with us. So let's not get involved. OK?"

My grandfather turned away and started hacking at the scanner again.

I sat down at the kitchen table, opened my notebook, and added: "Reinstate Pluto's Planetary Status?" right underneath the polar bear entry on my Possible Passions list.

As they were leaving, Chancellor Fontana and Ms. Helen mentioned that they thought it would be a "good idea" for us to "stick close to the apartment" for a while. Just to be safe.

I'm sure the two Martian police officers they posted outside the door were just a formality.

Sylvie retreated to her room, muttering something about getting more beauty rest. I could have sworn she had my grandfather's iPad hidden underneath her sweatshirt, but she shut and locked the door behind her before I could make sure.

My grandfather spent the rest of the day muttering at the DNA scanner and occasionally throwing things across the kitchen. Which meant that I had nothing to do but play soccer with Elliot and Venetio in the living room.

Soccer is nearly impossible when you have a tail. By the time I finally gave up, I had shattered two lamps and both of my palms had rug burn from having to break my fall so often.

I sat down on the couch to watch Venetio teach Elliot the basics of being a soccer goalie.

Venetio was not particularly athletic. And even with his cold suit, he was constantly overheating and having to take breaks. But still, he seemed to know what he was talking about. He ran Elliot through a series of drills and then installed him in front of a make-shift goal, consisting of an overturned couch with two armchairs on top of it.

"A good goalie knows how to anticipate a shot," Venetio explained, dribbling a soccer ball toward Elliot. When he pulled his foot back and kicked, the shot went right into the goal before Elliot had even moved.

"Anticipate? How do I do that?" Elliot asked, retrieving the ball and tossing it back.

"You've got to guess where I'm going to kick it," Venetio answered, coming toward the goal again, this time faking to the left before he cut right. "And you've got to make your move before I even kick the ball, or it'll be too late."

This time, Elliot dove to the left and barely managed to swat Venetio's shot away from the goal before landing facedown on the carpet.

"Better," Venetio said.

"Thanks," Elliot gasped from the floor.

"It's really a pity you could never play for Pluto," Venetio added.

"Because of the DNA tests?" I asked, remembering what Sylvie had said.

"Yeah. Everybody's so nuts about gene-ing these days that they test a drop of every player's blood before he or she takes the field," Venetio explained. "If your DNA isn't fifty-one percent from the planet you're representing, you can't play."

A second soccer ball sailed past Venetio's head and toward the goal. It hit one of the armchairs with a solid *thunk* and sent it spinning.

Then a third ball hit the second armchair, sending it spinning in the opposite direction.

"Wow," Elliot said, still on the floor. "You're not bad."

"Not bad?" Sylvie repeated from the doorway. She was keeping a third ball up in the air, bouncing it on her knee, then the inside of her foot, then the top of her other foot, then back again. She made it look easy. "I'm way better than not bad. I was a phenom! I was the youngest member of the Red Razers in Martian history. They had to rewrite laws so I could play. I'm awesome."

"You're OK," Elliot allowed, standing up and assuming what Venetio had called the "ready stance": legs apart, hands up.

Sylvie just laughed and switched legs, keeping the ball bouncing.

"Venetio's right about anticipating. When it doubt, go to your right. Most soccer players are right-footed. And most right-footed players tend to kick to their left—which is your right. And lefties tend to shoot to their right, your left."

"But you're left-footed," Elliot pointed out. "And you just shot in both directions."

"I said we *tend* to do certain things. Not that we *always* do."

And as if to prove her point, she did a blink-and-you'd-miss-it jump kick, firing the ball directly at Elliot's middle.

He caught it and doubled over, grunting loudly.

"Ugh," Elliot grunted. "Soccer's a lot rougher than I thought it would be."

Sylvie giggled.

"I'll bet Venetio hasn't even told you about sudden death yet."

"Sudden...what?" I asked.

"Death," Venetio said calmly. "It's not really what it sounds like. In every ISF game, there are two random, one-minute periods when if anybody makes a goal, their team wins the game. Regardless of what the score was before the period started."

"It's supposed to make the game more exciting," Sylvie explained.

"If the sudden death periods are random, how do you know when you're in one?" I asked.

Sylvie and Venetio both snorted with laughter. Elliot and I exchanged puzzled looks.

"Trust me," Sylvie said finally. "You know when you're in sudden death."

"Great news!" my grandfather interrupted, running in from the kitchen. "I've gotten a little bit more range on the scanner. A few more hours, I think, and I'll have it up and running so we can find out where that lab is."

"No need," Sylvie said, holding up the iPad. "I already found it."

Thank Goodness for the Nerds

I've been looking for that," my grandfather muttered irritably as Sylvie set the iPad down on the coffee table.

She shrugged an apology as we all gathered around the screen.

"This is a geologic survey of Mars," she explained. "If Sunder Labs is here, it has to be somewhere hidden. We didn't pick up anything on the short-range scanner this morning on the tour, so we know that they're not downtown. And I don't think they can be in any of the existing tunnels, or someone would have found them by now. Which means they must have dug out a space of their own."

"OK, but where?" Elliot asked, squinting at the map. "Mars is pretty big. They could be anywhere."

"Not quite," Sylvie corrected him, then looked over at my grandfather. "You said they're having money problems, right?"

"Right," my grandfather answered, sounding like he wasn't quite sure where she was going with this.

"Which means they would need to dig someplace cheap. If I was a secret lab with money problems, there is one really obvious place I'd dig," Sylvie said, pointing to a blob of orange in the western corner of the map. "It's close to the surface, so it wouldn't have to be very deep. And this pocket is composed entirely of lacustrine sediment, which is a really cheap type of rock to dig through."

"How do you know that?" I asked.

"I googled it," she replied.

My grandfather squinted down at the map, absently rubbing his neck with one hand.

"Why not over here?" He pointed to another blob of orange. "There's that sediment stuff over here too, right?"

"Yes, but it's too close to Central. People would have noticed if there was digging going on there. Over here would be way smarter," Sylvie said, her finger tapping the orange blob she had pointed to originally. "It's the only large area close to the surface that is almost entirely free of either iron ore or peridotite."

She looked up triumphantly, and I could only stare at her.

"You definitely weren't getting your beauty rest just now, were you?" I asked.

"Nope," she agreed and then gave me a hard look. "Why? Do you think I need some?"

"Er, no," I mumbled, not quite sure what she wanted me to say. Was Sylvie asking me if I thought she was pretty? I had never really thought of her as pretty or not pretty or anything like that. She was just...Sylvie.

"If you're right, Sylvie," my grandfather said, still sounding a bit hesitant. "And if the lab is where you say it is, then we'll have to go up to the surface to get there."

"Cool," Elliot whispered, nudging me in the ribs.

"Let's see now," my grandfather said. "I think I have enough sushi left to bribe the police officers outside the door. The surface though…"

"Is it hard to get there?" I asked, suddenly a little bit worried. I was just as excited as Elliot to see the surface of Mars up close.

My grandfather shrugged.

"That depends on how much Earth candy Sylvie has left in that pocket of hers."

"Only two kinds of folks go up to the surface," said the suspicious Martian proprietor of the rental spaceship shop on the outskirts of Mars Central. "Miners and homesteaders. And you lot don't look like either of those."

"We're the third kind. The kind that doesn't want any questions asked," my grandfather said, as Sylvie handed the Martian two boxes of Wild Cherry and Watermelon Nerds.

The rental Martian's eyes bulged.

"Are these real?" he asked, carefully inspecting the boxes.

"In all of their artificially flavored, illegal glory," my grandfather assured him, winking at Sylvie. Most Earth candy was illegal in Mars. It hadn't really occurred to me until then that by arriving here with her usual pocket stash, Sylvie officially qualified as a smuggler.

The rental Martian opened one of the boxes and brought it up to his nose. He inhaled deeply, smiled, and handed my grandfather a set of keys.

"No questions here."

The Martian was so excited by the Nerds that he threw in our rental space suits for free. They looked a lot like large trash bags with sleeves—until we put them on and they instantly suctioned to our bodies, forming a skin-tight barrier between our skin and the inhospitable Martian atmosphere. They even covered my plates, my tail, and my spikes. The suits all came with helmets that could collapse into the neck of the suit and then shoot up over our heads again with the touch of a button.

"Are you sure you don't need one?" I asked Venetio, who had declined his trash bag.

"Nah," he said. "Like I said, Plutonians need far less oxygen than Earthlings or Martians. I can breathe just fine on the surface."

"But the rest of you can't," the rental Martian warned us. "You've got about four hours of breathable air in the ship, plus two built into your suits. Don't lose track of time, or you'll suffocate and die. Enjoy your trip!"

Our ship, which had the name *Sabatier* painted boldly on the outside, was made to seat eight people. So the five of us had more than enough space as we flew up and out of the Valles Marineris canyon and started making our way west.

We used up an hour of breathable air getting to the spot Sylvie had marked on the map. Up close, Mars was the same tomato-soup orange it had been from space. The sky above us was yellowy-pink and surprisingly bright. We passed at least a half-dozen mining camps and a few smaller clumps of circular tents, which Sylvie said were called "habs."

I wouldn't say that the surface was exactly crowded. There were miles of open space between the small pockets of civilization, but there was a lot more up here than I had thought.

"How did we miss all of this stuff?" I wondered out loud, mostly to myself.

"Huh?" Sylvie asked. She was sitting across from me in the main part of the ship. Elliot was next to me, facing Venetio. My grandfather was in the front seat, driving.

"NASA has sent all kinds of things to Mars," I told her. "Like rovers and orbiters and stuff. But nothing ever recorded anything like the habs."

"Sure they did," Sylvie said, yawning hugely. "There's a whole division of Martian-Earthling relations whose job is to alter any digital image transmitted from Mars to Earth."

"Alter?" Elliot asked.

"Yeah, you know. Like Photoshop? It's pretty easy. My dad says the technology you guys send is always pretty low quality."

"But they miss stuff sometimes," Elliot pointed out. "Like the face. And the pyramid! And just before we left, I was reading about this thing that looked like a bone—"

"Oh yeah, those. My dad also says that some of the Martian-Earthling Affairs guys have a pretty weird sense of humor."

Venetio snorted as the spaceship began to slow down. My grandfather turned around from the front seat.

"Everybody put your helmets up," he said. "We're here."

The coolest part about walking on the surface of Mars was definitely the lower-gravity thing.

The boots the rental guy gave us did not come with the gravity inserts that we'd all been wearing in our shoes since we got to Mars. So we were all bouncing along like crazy as we followed my grandfather away from the ship.

"Basketball up here would be a-mazing!" Elliot enthused as he launched himself into the air.

My grandfather shushed him and motioned for us all to look at the screen of the short-range DNA scanner. I was pretty sure the mask part of my helmet was designed for someone with eye problems; it was really blurry. All I could see on the screen were a lot of crisscrossing lines, some wavy things that looked like interference…and a very tiny, flashing blip in the lower right-hand corner.

"This way!" my grandfather announced, turning slightly to the right and marching straight over an orangey dune. "The signal will be clearer once we get underground. We need to find an entrance."

Just a few dunes away, we found one. I had assumed that the entrance to an ultra-secret research lab would look, I don't know, at least vaguely high-tech. But the entrance we found was a straight-up cave. Not even a cave, really. More like a hole in the ground.

A hole that was being guarded by half a dozen human guards, all wearing space suits and helmets and carrying large, complicated-looking guns.

We all ducked behind the nearest dune before we could be seen.

"I was right," Sylvie whispered urgently, punching Elliot in the arm.

"Ow!" he exclaimed, rubbing his shoulder. "I never said you weren't!"

"This does look like the place," my grandfather said, setting down the DNA scanner and unshouldering a large canvas bag. "Human sentries. Heavy security. And Mr. Juarez's DNA signature is most definitely somewhere beneath our feet."

"So what now?" Venetio asked.

"Yeah," I said. "How are we going to get in without anybody noticing us?"

"We're not," my grandfather said simply. He unzipped the bag and looked over at me, a slight smile visible through his helmet's face shield.

"Have you seen Star Wars?"

The Death Star
(No, Not Really)

This is perfect," Elliot effused, beaming as my grandfather handed him a white lab coat. "You're Han Solo, right? And I'm Luke, obviously. And, Sawyer, you're…well…"

"Chewbacca," I finished for him. "You can say it. I'm the Wookiee."

"No, you're not," my grandfather said, handing Sylvie a lab coat as well. I noticed that he had not brought one for me.

"You kind of are," Elliot said with an apologetic grin. "I mean, they got around inside the Death Star by pretending Chewie was their prisoner, right?"

"Sawyer is not a prisoner," my grandfather said firmly. "He's an escaped research subject. And only for the duration of this mission."

"Swell," I muttered. At least no one was suggesting I wear handcuffs.

Elliot turned to Sylvie next.

"And you're Leia," he informed her.

"I am so *not* Leia!" Sylvie retorted, giving him an angry look as she tried to roll up the sleeves of her lab coat. It was still far too big. She was practically swimming in white fabric.

"Sure you are—" Elliot started.

"Leia was the one they were going to rescue," Sylvie pointed out. "Nobody is rescuing me, are they? I want to be Luke."

"You can't be Luke. I'm already Luke."

"You can't just call it like that. It's not shotgun. It's—"

"What about me?" Venetio interrupted. "Who am I?"

Elliot, Sylvie, and I exchanged questioning looks. Venetio was wearing his lab coat and also Sylvie's sweatshirt, hood up, to hide his blueness. I was pretty sure he had never seen Star Wars and had no idea what we were talking about. But he was looking up at us so eagerly from beneath the folds of the floppy hood that I felt a twinge at how badly he wanted to be a part of things.

"Venetio can be R2-D2," my grandfather pronounced, with conversation-ending authority. "Now let's get moving."

Getting into the cave—er, hole—was actually easy. All it took was Sylvie's last six boxes of Nerds, and my grandfather's shame-faced request that he and his team be allowed to return the escaped research subject (me) to the lab before anybody noticed.

I just looked down at my feet, trying to look busted. Sylvie and Elliot stood on either side of me wearing their lab coats and keeping a firm grip on both of my arms, trying to look like stern scientists. And Venetio brought up the rear, hiding under Sylvie's sweatshirt and trying to look less blue.

The laboratory looked pretty much like how I had pictured Mars before I had seen the steel-and-glass underground city with my own eyes: dark and cramped. It was basically a series of tunnels that no one had bothered to smooth over and make pretty. My grandfather walked confidently down the widest one, DNA scanner in hand, and the rest of us marched after him. Strings of bare lightbulbs followed us, giving us just enough light to see by.

Other tunnels stretched out to either side of the main one. Two scientists, both wearing white lab coats and helmets, came out of one rather suddenly, and I'm pretty sure my heart skipped a beat.

But they just continued on their way, sidestepping us and continuing their conversation as though there was nothing unusual about us being here at all.

We passed a few more scientists, who paid us no more attention. I was just starting to relax and to think that we might be able to pull this off, when we rounded a corner and came face-to-face with a giant, metal door.

We all froze. My grandfather let out a puzzled "Hmmm" and frowned at the numbered keypad beside the lock.

"I think we need a code to get in here," he whispered. "Let's try to find a way around."

"But—" Sylvie began, then stopped abruptly as another scientist came around the corner behind us.

He was human and just slightly shorter than my grandfather. He stopped behind Venetio and stood patiently, like someone waiting for an elevator on Earth.

Oh no, I said to myself, and my inner voice started to sound panicky, *he's waiting for us to open the door.*

After a moment or two of awkward silence, he looked up and addressed my grandfather, who was closest to the keypad.

"Got your hands full?" he asked.

"Er, yeah," my grandfather said, holding up the DNA scanner and motioning to me.

"I got it," the scientist said, smiling good-naturedly as he stepped forward and punched a code into the pad.

The door opened with a loud, mechanical squeak. We all followed the scientist inside to a cramped metal room. The door shut behind us. Then there was a loud whirring sound and a sudden blast of air.

After a moment, a green light flashed above our heads. An oddly soothing voice came over the loudspeaker: *Pressurization achieved.*

The scientist removed his helmet without hesitation, and the rest of us hurried to copy him. The air was a little bit thinner than I was used to. It was breathable, but it tasted funny and gave me a little bit of a headache. I took a couple of very deep breaths, relieved that my head was no longer in the confines of the space suit.

Unfortunately, without our helmets, the scientist could see us all a lot more clearly. And judging from his wide eyes, he was a bit startled to find himself in close quarters with two tall humans, a Martian, a Plutonian, and a dinosaur-Earthling hybrid.

A second door, on the other side of the tiny room, started to swing open. The scientist dove for it, but my grandfather was too quick for him. In one smooth move, he tossed the DNA scanner to Elliot (who caught it), tucked the scientist into a firm headlock, and got a hand over his mouth.

"We need to hurry," he said urgently.

Sylvie ripped the scanner out of Elliot's hands and sprinted out of the chamber. Elliot, Venetio, and I followed her. My grandfather came along behind us, dragging the scientist, who was making muffled yelling sounds.

This area of the lab was nicer than the first part. The floors and walls were made out of metal, and the lights above our heads were normal, rectangular fluorescent fixtures instead of naked lightbulbs. We made a terrible racket as we jogged down a series of hallways, following Sylvie. I picked my tail up in one hand and tried to ignore the uncomfortable bouncing of my plates.

"Someone's gonna see us!" Elliot whispered urgently.

"We're almost there!" Sylvie yelled over her shoulder, making no attempt to be quiet.

Two sharp turns later, she stopped abruptly in front of a metal door with the number thirty-nine stamped on it.

"Here! He's in here!" Sylvie announced, holding up the beeping scanner.

Elliot shook his head.

"I've got a bad feeling about this," he said to no one in particular as Sylvie twisted the doorknob.

The room was pretty big. It had several long, low tables that were covered in chemistry equipment. There were stools to sit on, several sinks, and an emergency eyewash station in the corner. Just like our science lab at school.

But unlike our science lab, there were also four large hospital beds lined up against one wall.

Only one other person was in the room. He was wearing a helmet, but it had a clear face shield, so I could see most of him. He was blurry, but I recognized the glasses and the bad comb-over from the Missing picture on the giant screen downtown.

Mr. Juarez.

But even as Sylvie gave a small yelp of joy and started running toward him, my tail gave an uncomfortable twitch. I had caught Elliot's bad feeling. Something was wrong.

It took me only a moment to figure out what it was: his helmet.

Why would Mr. Juarez be wearing a helmet in a pressurized area?

The door behind us opened again. There was a loud hissing sound, and suddenly the room was filled with the scent of fresh lemons. But there was another smell too. Somewhere beneath the lemons, a sickeningly familiar sweet stench entered my nostrils. I covered my nose and mouth with my hand, but it was too late. My head had already started to swim.

I turned clumsily in the direction of the door. And my hazy mind saw a fleeting image of a bony frill and three distinctive horns…before I lost my balance and the world went dark.

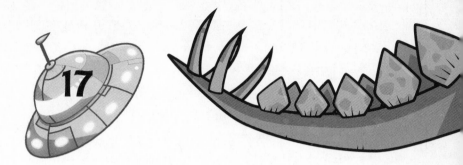

Busted

I woke up to a sharp pain in my arm.

"Ow!" I cried. I tried to wrench my arm away, only to find that it was strapped down to the hospital bed I was lying on. My other arm, both legs, and my tail were all tied down with cloth restraints as well. There was something like a giant rubber band around my middle, carefully threaded through my plates, that was keeping me pinned down in a weird position, half on my side.

My space suit had been removed and my shirtsleeve had been rolled up. The scientist from the elevator was looming over me, aiming an alarmingly big hypodermic syringe at my exposed arm.

"Sorry," he said. "I missed again. Fifth time's the charm though, right?"

I could have sworn he grinned as he stabbed the needle into my arm again.

This time he didn't miss; he slipped the needle into my vein and taped it into place, just like the time Dr. Bakker had taken my blood to test me for anemia.

"Ah. You're awake."

The triceratops head from my hazy, pre-fainting vision appeared over the scientist's shoulder, just as the bed started moving underneath me. The top part went up and the bottom part tipped toward the floor until I was pretty much straight up and down. The straps holding me in place kept me from sliding onto the floor.

Now that I was upright, I could see we were in the same laboratory we had ran into, right before we had been knocked out. I couldn't move my head very much, but I could see that the other three beds were occupied by my grandfather, Elliot, and Venetio. They were still unconscious.

Where was Sylvie?

"You see, Asaph? They're coming around. It shouldn't be long now."

The scientist from the elevator took the needle out of my arm, slapped a Band-Aid over the dot of blood on the inside of my elbow, and left the room. Now that his head was out of the way, I was able to get a good look at the triceratops. Good enough to see that he wasn't a full triceratops.

The hands sticking out of the sleeves of his white lab coat were human. His head was human too, except for the two horns above his eyes and the slightly larger horn where his nose should be. There was also a huge, bony frill framing his head. It looked sort of like an over-sized Elizabethan collar. Or the plastic thing (which my dad called the "cone of shame") that Fanny had to wear once so she couldn't lick her stitches.

Triceratops Man was facing me so I couldn't tell if he had a tail or not. But I was guessing he did. His eyes, small and beady, were focused on me. But it didn't seem like he had been talking to me.

I craned my neck to see over his shoulder. Mr. Juarez was sitting at one of the lab tables. His helmet was off now. And an even shorter Martian was propped up on a stool beside him with her head down on the table.

Sylvie.

"If *he's* awake, then why isn't *she* awake?" Mr. Juarez asked Triceratops Man, patting Sylvie worriedly on the head, right between her antennae.

"It shouldn't be long now," Triceratops Man repeated. "She'll be awake in moments."

"Or not," I couldn't resist adding.

Mr. Juarez looked up in alarm. Triceratops Man narrowed his already really narrow eyes at me.

I shrugged. I had recognized the smell beneath the lemons.

"Good Girl and Good Boy sprays are unpredictable on hybrids," I informed them. It was even written on the can. And Sylvie and I had proved it the time Principal Mathis sprayed us with it when she tried to kidnap Elliot.

Triceratops Man turned his back to me—he did have a tail! No spikes though—and picked up something from the table that Mr. Juarez and Sylvie were sitting at.

He turned back to me and held up a tiny, midnight-blue bottle.

"Good Boy and Good Girl sprays are Amalgam Lab products. This is Good Riddance spray. One of ours. The base formula is, er, similar.

But we've eliminated the hybrid variability and made a number of other improvements. I'm sure you noticed the lemony-fresh scent."

Before I could even think of how to respond to that, there was a loud groan from the bed closest to me.

My grandfather stirred, pulled for a second against his restraints, and then groaned again.

Triceratops Man pushed a button and brought my grandfather's bed up like mine so he could look him square in the face.

"Ah, Gavin," Triceratops Man said. "So glad you could join us."

I wasn't sure I'd ever heard anyone use my grandfather's first name before. And it sounded weird, especially coming from a dinosaur in a lab coat. But my grandfather didn't seem to think it was strange that this hybrid knew his name.

"Hello, Otto," my grandfather said grumpily.

"Always a pleasure to see you, Gavin. I assume this little stealth mission of yours means you're not going to take me up on my offer of employment?"

"As I've told you before," my grandfather said, "I will not work for you. Not now, not ever."

"Never hurts to keep asking," Triceratops Man muttered and then turned away to bring Elliot and Venetio's beds to standing positions. They were both awake and wearing identical expressions of wide-eyed confusion.

I looked questioningly over at my grandfather.

"Dr. Marsh—Otto—and I used to work at Amalgam Labs together," he explained. "Then he left to start Sunder Labs. I refused to leave with him."

"A poor choice," Triceratops Man—Dr. Marsh—interjected. "Which makes me very curious why you are here now."

My grandfather glared at him.

"Why do you think?"

Behind Dr. Marsh, Sylvie woke up and sat bolt upright on her stool.

"Dad!" she exclaimed. She looked overjoyed for a split second before she glanced around and saw what was going on. "Dad? What...? Why...?"

"Don't worry, Sylvie," Mr. Juarez said, putting a hand on her shoulder. "It's OK. Everything is going to be fine."

"But—but—what is he doing to my friends?" she demanded, throwing his hand off and standing up a little bit shakily.

"I'm just getting to know them better," Dr. Marsh assured her.

She turned, did a slight double take at his frill, and then squinted up at something over my head.

I craned my neck as far as it would go and noticed for the first time that there was a flat-screen TV monitor up there. Actually, there were four, one above each of our beds.

"Such fascinating friends you have, Ms. Juarez," Dr. Marsh said, following her gaze to my monitor. "A juvenile Earthling-stegosaurus hybrid."

He walked on, coming to my grandfather's bed. "An adult Earthling-stegosaurus hybrid, with his dinosaur genes suppressed."

He came to Venetio's bed and paused again.

"And a juvenile Plutonian. I'm sure he'll be most useful."

"You listen here," Venetio said angrily. "I have a game to get to, and I'll do whatever it takes to—"

There was a blast of air and a burst of lemon scent as Dr. Marsh aimed the tiny blue bottle directly in Venetio's face. I quickly closed my mouth and stopped breathing, as Venetio's eyes rolled back into his head and his chin drooped down to his chest.

"I've always like Plutonians better when they're unconscious," Dr. Marsh admitted. "He'll be fine in about an hour or so," he assured us before moving on to Elliot's bed.

"And finally, an Earthling. Human," he said. "A basic, run-of-the-mill, thoroughly uninteresting human."

"Hey!" Elliot exclaimed, looking offended before he remembered that he wasn't supposed to be breathing. He quickly closed his mouth again.

Dr. Marsh shrugged.

"Three out of four isn't too bad, I guess."

Sylvie narrowed her eyes at the hybrid scientist.

"Let. Them. Go."

Dr. Marsh looked surprised.

"Oh no, I couldn't possibly. They are much too valuable as research subjects. Well, except for the human. I've no interest in him."

"Hey!" Elliot muttered through pursed lips, trying not to open his mouth this time.

Dr. Marsh waved a hand in his direction.

"I'd happily let that one go. As a favor to Asaph's daughter."

"Why would you want to do a favor for my dad?" Sylvie asked. And when Dr. Marsh only smiled that odd triceratops grin at her, she turned to her father.

"You said you were coming back for me," she spat at him. I

could tell she was trying to sound mad, but she also sounded a bit like she was about to cry. "When I went to Earth with Mom, you said you were going to come and get me. But you never came. Why didn't you?"

"I explained it all in my note," Mr. Juarez told her. "Didn't you get it? I specifically told your mother to tell you—"

"—that you were being held against your will!" Sylvie finished for him. "I know, I read it! Parts of it anyway. You also told me not to worry. But come on, Dad, of course I'm going to worry when you say something like…"

She trailed off. Mr. Juarez was shaking his head sadly. And my brain, which probably should have caught this minutes ago, started to ask itself why he wasn't wearing handcuffs. Or leg restraints. In fact, there was nothing to indicate that he was being kept as a prisoner.

"No, Sylvie." He sighed. "What I actually said was that I wasn't being held against my will. I told you not to come after me."

Sylvie's mouth dropped open as Mr. Juarez exchanged a look with Dr. Marsh.

"The truth is, Sylvie, I didn't want you to come looking for me. I didn't need you to find me. Because I wasn't kidnapped and I wasn't lost. I'm exactly where I want to be."

Those Dang Nutri Nuggets

B ut...but..." Sylvie stammered. "But, Dad, this is a science lab. What are you doing in a science lab?"

Mr. Juarez cleared his throat.

"Dr. Marsh and I—that is to say, Sunder Labs and I—have a common interest. And we all thought it would be better if I remained here underground until our plan is complete—"

"Plan?" Sylvie demanded. "What plan? Dad, you're a restaurateur! You're not a scientist!" She turned to Dr. Marsh. "Don't you know he's not a scientist?"

Dr. Marsh chuckled but said nothing.

"I'm not here to do the science," said Mr. Juarez. "I'm what's called a backer."

"A what-er?"

"You see, Sylvie," Dr. Marsh interjected. "Sunder Labs is built on a foundation of ideas. Brilliant, groundbreaking, universe-changing ideas. But it takes money to bring ideas to life. And that's where we were coming up a little short."

Sylvie drew in a sharp breath.

"My father is giving you money?"

"Yes, I am," Mr. Juarez said. "I've invested a great deal of money in a specific Sunder Labs program called EGM."

"EGM?" my grandfather interjected. "You're not still trying to do that, are you?"

"Trying?" Dr. Marsh asked with a chuckle. "Why no, Gavin. We're not trying. We're doing."

"EGM?" I asked and exchanged a puzzled look with Elliot.

"It stands for elective genetic mutation," Dr. Marsh explained, sounding excited. "It's an idea I had way back when I was still at Amalgam. It involves using a virus to introduce specific, targeted genetic material into a subject."

"A virus?" I asked, thinking hard. The word had triggered something in my brain. Suddenly, I was back in Ms. Filch's class on the first day of fifth grade. And the voice of Dr. Dana from that lame Amalgam Labs video was echoing in my brain:

…we may never know exactly how the dinosaur-human hybrid serum was created. Or exactly who was responsible for injecting that serum into a virus and for putting that virus into the ice-cream maker in the laboratory's cafeteria…

I felt something very, very cold fall sharply into the pit of my stomach. And it wasn't ice cream.

"The dinosaur-human hybrids," I said breathlessly, looking over at my grandfather in horror. "Us. Dr. Marsh created…us?"

My grandfather nodded.

"Well, Amalgam Labs turned down my formal request for human subjects," Dr. Marsh said with an irritated snort. "They left me no choice. But I had every faith in the safety of the serum. Why else would I have included myself in the sample group?"

"Maybe because you thought the process would be easily reversible?" my grandfather suggested. "Which turned out to be incorrect."

Dr. Marsh coughed into his human hand.

"True, it didn't work out exactly as I had hoped. The cure took longer to work out than I had anticipated. Luckily, I had you to help me with that, Gavin."

"Wait a sec," I cut in. "If you know about the cure, then why didn't you take it? Why do you still have triceratops parts?"

"Oh, I never wanted the cure for myself," Dr. Marsh said, smiling as he stroked the edge of his frill. "You'd be amazed at the mileage I get out of this. Investors see me, and they open their wallets. And the money really starts flowing when I tell them that the dinosaur-human hybrids are only the beginning."

My grandfather's head snapped up.

"What?"

"Oh, the hybrids are old news, my friend. That was years ago. The real market is in subtle, targeted gene-ing. You want to be taller? There's a gene for that. Smarter? Faster? There're genes for those too. And we can sell them to you. And not only that, but we can now manipulate the genes themselves. We can turn them on, turn them off, tone them down, amp them up—you name it. We can fine-tune anything you want, fix anything you don't like about yourself."

My grandfather was shaking his head sadly.

"Otto, that's...that's terrible."

"Why?" Dr. Marsh demanded. "Why is it terrible? Why shouldn't everybody be exactly what they want to be? Provided they can afford it, of course."

"It's going too far," my grandfather said patiently. "You're messing around with things you don't understand completely. And besides, who are you going to sell it to? Gene-ing is illegal in Mars. Even elective gene-ing."

"It won't be," Dr. Marsh informed him. "Not under the Plutonians."

My grandfather was staring at Dr. Marsh. It looked to me like he was trying to figure out if the triceratops hybrid was insane or not.

I was wondering the same thing.

"Say again?" my grandfather asked with a glance over at Venetio, who was still out cold.

"You're right about one thing, Gavin," Dr. Marsh continued. "Now that we have a product that everybody wants, we need a market where we can legally sell it. Mars is ideal—a centrally located planet within easy shuttle distance from every other planet in the galaxy. But the current population is a bit...resistant to the idea of genetic alteration."

"The current population?" Sylvie asked suspiciously as Mr. Juarez started to fidget in his chair.

"The Plutonians, on the other hand, are far more open-minded about the possibilities of EGM. And coincidentally, they are looking for a new planet."

"But what about the Martians?" Sylvie asked.

"Oh, the Martians will still be here," Dr. Marsh answered. "They'll just be…changed."

"Changed?" I asked, and the bad feeling I had when we first saw Mr. Juarez came back with a vengeance.

"Yes. My dinosaur parts may have gotten us the investors we needed to fund EGM research, but we're going to need something more dramatic to take it to the next level. Something that will leave no doubt that when it comes to gene-ing, Sunder Labs can do anything. Even, say, turn a whole planet of Martians into Plutonians."

My mouth dropped open.

"You can't do that!" Sylvie exclaimed.

"Don't worry," Mr. Juarez assured her hurriedly. "They'll all get changed back. Once the Martian Council has agreed to turn the government over to the BURPSers, Dr. Marsh is going to turn them all back into Martians. Like nothing ever happened."

"But then the BURPSers will be in charge of Mars?" my grandfather asked.

"Exactly," Dr. Marsh said, sounding pleased. "The Martians can stay safe in their underground world, while the Plutonians colonize the surface. But it'll be the BURPSers who run the planet. Their first order of business will be to legalize gene-ing. And their second," he said with a glance at Mr. Juarez, "will be to outlaw Nutri Nuggets."

Sylvie's eyes bulged.

"That's why you're doing this?" she asked her father, as her lower lip started trembling. "Because of Nutri Nuggets?"

Mr. Juarez cleared his throat and looked straight at his daughter.

"Those Nutri Nuggets are putting my restaurants out of business," he said darkly. "Those stupid, disgusting nuggets are destroying every-thing I've worked for. Say what you like about Plutonians, they are much too into food to ever allow such nonsense on their planet. On a planet full of Plutonians, my restaurants won't just survive. They'll thrive."

Sylvie looked gobsmacked.

Mr. Juarez spread his hands.

"What was I supposed to do? Allow my entire life's work to crumble right before my eyes? The planet changed. I had to either evolve or die. I had no other choice."

"Everybody has a choice." I spoke up. "What you're doing is horribly wrong!"

"Oh, I wouldn't be too down on what we're doing here, Sawyer," Dr. Marsh scolded. "After all, you have your grandfather to thank for it."

"That is a lie, Otto!" my grandfather hissed. "An absolute lie. I will not allow my grandson to think I am responsible for any of this—"

"Oh, but you are, Gavin. It's the cure, you see. The one you and I created together at Amalgam. It turns out that the cure is the key to unlocking EGM."

◈◈◈

I was looking straight at my grandfather when Dr. Marsh said that, so I saw when all of the blood drained out of his face at once.

"You mean to tell me that you've based all of this"—my grandfa-ther waved a hand around, indicating the lab—"on the cure?"

"That's right," Dr. Marsh said proudly. "The cure helped us to develop EGM. And most importantly for the Martians, it'll be the cure that turns them back to normal once the planet changes hands. Easy-peasy, like nothing ever happened."

My grandfather started muttering to himself under his breath. I caught a couple of words, several of which I had once been grounded for saying out loud. When he finally got hold of himself, he looked severely at Dr. Marsh.

"Otto, there's something you need to know. EGM—"

Dr. Marsh held up his hand.

"Spare me your moral judgments, Gavin. I've never understood your eccentrically human hang-ups about doing the right thing. You're half dinosaur, you know. It's time you gave in to your baser instincts—"

Dr. Marsh continued talking. And Sylvie started yelling at her father.

"I can't believe I wrote a whole paper about you! I even called you my 'hero'! What a waste!"

The two distinct strings of conversation were starting to make my head hurt. Particularly because there was a third conversation taking place entirely in my own brain. And those words were the loudest of them all:

It's never a good sign when the bad guy tells you his plan.

Dr. Marsh had told us what he was planning to do. Maybe not all the details—I still had no idea how he would possibly gene an entire planet. But he had told us he was going to do it. And that meant he had no plans to let us go.

If we were going to get out of here, we were going to have to get ourselves out.

I pulled uselessly against my restraints and looked around the lab. It was full of lab equipment. Tons of things that were sharp, breakable, and possibly even explosive. But only if I could get to them. And I really didn't see how I was going to do that when I couldn't move more than an inch or two.

Dr. Marsh had left the bottle of Good Riddance spray on the table, just out of Sylvie's reach. She would be able to get it, but only if she stood up and slid a few feet down the table. And there was no way she'd be able to do either of those things without Dr. Marsh or her father seeing.

"You've got to listen to me, Otto," my grandfather was thundering. "There are things you don't know—"

"Fewer and fewer every day!" Dr. Marsh proclaimed.

The closest thing to my bed was the emergency eyewash station. Right next to that, there was a fire extinguisher, an oxygen tank, a flame-retardant suit, and a giant red button that said PRESS ONLY IN EVENT OF MAJOR CHEMICAL SPILL.

I had no idea what would happen if that button got pushed. But I was willing to bet it would be noisy, dramatic, and disruptive. Which all seemed like pretty good things right then.

Unfortunately, the button was a good six feet away from my bed. Which was about five feet and ten inches farther than I was currently able to reach.

My grandfather was still trying to get a word in edgewise with Dr. Marsh.

"If you would just shut up for two seconds—"

"You know what your problem is, Gavin? You're too

narrow-minded. You're so focused on the minutiae that you never see the big picture—"

I pulled on my stupid restraints again. My spikes would have cut through them in two seconds. The way my tail was tied down, my tennis balls were actually just barely within reach of my right hand. But the spikes themselves were too far away and tied down at too weird of an angle to cut anything.

But I could reach the tennis balls, I thought. At least one of them. Possibly two.

Moving very slowly, I stretched my right arm as far as I could. My fingers closed around the nearest ball. After a few seconds of fumbling, I was able to work it off the spike.

It came off into my hand with a soft *pop*.

I looked around worriedly. But no one had heard.

The ball was losing air fast, so I quickly took aim and fired it toward the MAJOR CHEMICAL SPILL button.

It hit the word SPILL, an inch below the button, and bounced harmlessly to the floor.

I froze, certain everybody had seen that. After a second, I looked around.

My grandfather and Dr. Marsh were still yelling at each other. Elliot and Mr. Juarez were watching them argue, and Venetio was still unconscious.

But Sylvie had seen my throw. She nodded encouragingly at me and inched slightly closer to the spray bottle.

"…no sense of genetic destiny…" Dr. Marsh was saying accusingly.

I reached for the second tennis ball. It was farther away. My fingertips barely brushed the top of it. I strained with all of my might, so hard I was afraid I was going to rip my wrist out of joint. But I kept straining until I got all four fingers around the ball and was able to use my thumb to force it slowly upward.

Pop.

This time I aimed just slightly higher than I had before.

Escape from the Death Star (Really)

Red lights started flashing from the corners of the room. And a calm, robotic woman's voice came over the loudspeaker:

Attention. Hazardous chemical containment procedures have been activated. This area will be sealed off in sixty seconds.

Then an alarm started blaring. It was so loud that I desperately wanted to cover my ears, but I was still tied down.

Luckily, Sylvie wasn't. In one smooth movement she lunged for the bottle of Good Riddance spray and let loose two quick blasts directly in Dr. Marsh's face.

The trihorned scientist had no idea what hit him. His eyes rolled back and his legs collapsed underneath him. When he fell to the ground, his head lolled strangely against the side of his frill.

"Sylvie!" Mr. Juarez admonished, looking shocked.

"Sylvie, undo our restraints," my grandfather commanded. "We've got to get out of here."

"Don't even think about it, Sylvie," Mr. Juarez said threateningly, putting himself between Sylvie and my grandfather. "You're already in enough trouble as it is."

Sylvie looked back and forth between the two of them.

"Sylvie," my grandfather said calmly, "if we don't get out of here before they seal this wing, we'll never get out of this lab."

The alarm paused so that the robotic voice could be heard again:

This area will be sealed off in forty-five seconds.

Sylvie dodged her dad and leaped toward my grandfather. His arm restraints came off with a long *riiiiiip* of Velcro. She left him to bend down and unstrap his own legs while she ripped off my arm restraints, then Elliot's and Venetio's.

I unstrapped my legs and tail and nearly fell over, feeling light-headed as the blood suddenly rushed back into my tail.

Venetio fell forward and landed on his face. Elliot bent to help him, and Venetio looked up at him, confused.

"What happened?" he mumbled.

"I'll tell you later!" Elliot promised, pulling the Plutonian to his feet.

This area will be sealed off in thirty seconds.

"Sylvie—" Mr. Juarez said, wringing his hands.

"No!" Sylvie put up a hand. "I don't want anything to do with you!"

My grandfather grabbed her by the shoulders and pushed her toward the door.

"Run!" he said urgently. "You too, Asaph! Let's go!"

"What about—" I gestured at unconscious Dr. Marsh.

"He'll be fine," my grandfather said, and he grabbed our space suits with one hand as he shoved me toward the door with the other.

We ran.

The hallway outside was empty of people and bathed in red flashing lights. We sprinted back the way we had come. With his long legs, Elliot led the way, followed closely by Sylvie and her dad. My grandfather was next, looking anxiously over his shoulder at me. Venetio and I, with our short legs and jiggly dinosaur parts (respectively), brought up the rear.

This area will be sealed off in fifteen seconds.

"Look!" Elliot yelled, pointing.

A wall was coming down in the hallway in front of us. A disturbingly solid, metal wall that was probably capable of keeping microscopically small chemical particles from getting into the rest of the lab. It would have no problem keeping us sealed in here. And it really didn't look like the wall was going to take fifteen seconds to reach the floor.

Elliot reached it first and ducked underneath. Sylvie and her dad dove after him. My grandfather went next, reaching an arm back underneath toward me. The wall was just a few feet above the floor now, just barely higher than my knees.

"Come on, Sawyer!"

I was never one of those kids who played baseball. But my sprint to the wall and my feet-first slide underneath were like a textbook slide into home plate. It was beautiful.

Or, it would have been if I hadn't had seventeen plates on my back to slow me down.

Each plate killed my momentum just a tiny bit. I ran out of steam entirely when my chest was directly underneath the wall. I watched, frozen, as the bottom of the wall came down at me like a giant guillotine blade.

Then Venetio slammed into me from behind, hitting me square in the shoulders with both of his feet and shoving me the rest of the way to the other side.

I rolled over on my belly, grimacing at the pain in my squished plates. My grandfather and Elliot each grabbed one of Venetio's feet and yanked him under the wall—which came crashing down to the floor, slicing at least an inch of blond hair from the top of the Plutonian's head.

Please proceed away from the sealed area.

"Sure thing," Sylvie muttered and reached down a hand to help me up.

◊◊◊

"Ouch," Sylvie said, looking at my plates.

I couldn't see them for myself, but I could tell that several of them had been bent at strange angles. Normally, jamming one of my plates felt like stubbing a toe. But my heart was beating too fast and my blood was pumping too hard for me to notice much at the moment.

"We need to get back to the surface," my grandfather announced and looked us over with chagrin. All of us, except for Sylvie, had been divested of our lab coats when Dr. Marsh had tried to make us research subjects. We stuck out now like sore thumbs—tall, blue, dinosaur-shaped thumbs. Anyone who saw us would know instantly that we didn't belong.

And despite the fact that the mechanical voice was reminding us every fifteen seconds or so to *stay clear of the contaminated area*, it was only a matter of time before someone came to check out what had happened.

"None of you are going anywhere," Mr. Juarez snarled. And before anybody could move to stop him, he pressed a button on the wall.

"Escaped prisoners! I have escaped prisoners here on level two, right next to the—"

He trailed off as he noticed that my grandfather was pointing his six-shooter directly at his chest.

Mr. Juarez swallowed and looked nervously down the barrel of the gun.

"You can go," he said to my grandfather, pointing to him, Elliot, Venetio, and me, "but Sylvie is staying with me."

"Dad!" Sylvie exclaimed. "You were the one who told me not to come here in the first place!"

"Yes, I did. And now I'm telling you that you can't leave."

"I hear footsteps!" Venetio warned us. "Someone's coming!"

"Dad, you know this is wrong," Sylvie said. "What the lab is doing—it's wrong! I'm not staying here and neither should you. Come with us."

Mr. Juarez just shook his head.

"They're getting closer!" Venetio reported, bouncing up and down in agitation.

My grandfather sighed and then looked at Sylvie.

"We don't have time for this. Sylvie, it's your choice. Do you want to stay here with your father?"

"No," Sylvie said emphatically.

My grandfather nodded, pulled the trigger, and shot Mr. Juarez square in the chest.

"Dad!" Sylvie screamed as her father slumped against the lab wall and flopped over onto the ground.

She made as if to go to him, but my grandfather grabbed her arm.

"He's only stunned," he assured her and held up his gun. "Retrofitted with stun capacity."

He let go of her and took two enormous strides down the hallway. Then he paused when he realized that the rest of us had not moved.

"What? You didn't think I'd *kill* him?" He shook his head, looking horrified at the notion. "Come on, let's get out of here!"

I looked over at Sylvie. She was standing perfectly still, just staring down at her father. A little bit like my grandfather had shot her with the stun gun instead.

"Which way?" Elliot asked nervously.

"I doubt it matters," Venetio said gloomily. We were at a sort of crossroads of hallways, and footsteps were coming at us from at least three directions.

Sylvie raised her eyes up from her father and fixed them on the wall in front of her.

"Come on, Sylvie," I said, reaching down and taking a tentative grip at her hand, a little bit afraid that she was about to explode. Or cry. Or just never stop staring at the wall.

Instead, her head snapped up. She looked first at me, then down each of the hallways, then back to the wall in front of her. There was a large air vent there, right at knee level.

She backed up two steps, lunged forward, and put her foot right through the vent.

The rectangular screen, about the size of an oven door, crumpled beneath her foot. One more kick, and it disappeared entirely into the dark space of wall behind it.

Sylvie waved us all toward the hole.

"Into the air duct, boys."

Apparently, Sylvie was a little bit Leia after all.

I'm not even going to try and explain the difficulties of navigating an air vent shaft when you have plates, a tail, and four long spikes, only two of which are capped with tennis balls. The loose spikes got caught on everything in sight, which means it took me at least twice as long to crawl through the tiny, enclosed space as it would have for a normal person.

I was relieved when we finally made it into some sort of boiler room where we were able to put our space suits back on.

It was very lucky the rental Martian had given us the suits that had the built-in helmets. Otherwise, I don't know what we would have done when we reached the unpressurized area, and even less of an idea what would have happened when we tumbled back out onto the surface of Mars.

We came out of a small opening in the rock, just a few hundred meters from the hole where we had bribed our way inside.

The armed guards were still there. So were quite a few scientists, all wearing lab coats and helmets. They saw us at pretty much the same time we saw them.

I couldn't hear what they were saying. The surface of Mars was eerily silent on the other side of my helmet. But several of the scientists pointed in our direction, and the entire group turned as one and started running toward us like a herd of wildebeests in space helmets.

"This way!" my grandfather yelled. "The ship's not far!"

He was right. The ship was only a few dunes away. But it was not alone. Another herd of white-coated, helmeted scientists swarmed around our tiny, rented shuttle. When they saw us, they started running toward us as well.

"Now what?" Sylvie asked.

"I—I don't—" my grandfather stammered. He was holding his stun gun, but I knew it wouldn't be much help against the gangs of scientists that were now coming at us from two directions.

This was it. I was going to be held prisoner at a secret lab under the surface of Mars for the rest of my life. I was doomed to an eternity as a lab rat.

I was just starting to feel the first surges of real, honest-to-goodness panic welling up inside me when the wind whipped up and a ship came down right in front of us.

Once the enormous cloud of reddish Martian dust had cleared, I saw that the ship was even smaller than the one we had rented. When the roof popped open, only the driver's seat was occupied. And the face looking out at us from the other side of the helmet shield was familiar, even if her eyes were slightly angrier than they usually were.

"Mom?" Sylvie exclaimed.

Busted Again

As soon as we had taken off—leaving the two converging herds of angry scientists behind us—and the inside of the shuttle had pressurized itself, Mrs. Juarez whipped off her helmet.

"Where is it?" she demanded.

"What?" Sylvie asked, wearing a mask of wide-eyed innocence.

I removed my helmet as well and hesitantly took a deep breath of stale, space shuttle air.

Mrs. Juarez leaned over, keeping one hand on the controls and using the other to pat down the pockets on the sides of Sylvie's space suit.

The two of them were sitting in the front seats, while Elliot, my grandfather, Venetio, and I were squished into the tiny row of seats behind them.

"Hey!" Sylvie exclaimed when her mother's hand emerged, fingers triumphantly clenched around Sylvie's phone. "That's mine! You can't—"

"Quiet, *corazón*!" Mrs. Juarez snapped, dropping the cell phone into her purse and closing the clasp with an ominous snap. "When I gave you that phone, you made me a very specific promise. Do you remember what it was?"

Instead of answering, Sylvie crossed her arms and looked out the spaceship window.

"That you would always, without exception, answer my calls," Mrs. Juarez reminded her. "Which you have failed to do for the last three days. Privilege revoked, Sylvia!"

"Busted," Elliot muttered under his breath.

I put a hand over my mouth before a hysterical giggle could get out.

"Fine!" Sylvie yelled back. "I don't want that stupid old phone anyway!"

"Good, because you're not getting it back until you prove to me that you're old enough to handle the responsibility. And believe me, *mi hija*, leaving the planet without so much as a courtesy text is not what I mean by that! If I hadn't installed that GPS chip, I never would have—"

"What? You chipped me? That's an invasion of privacy! I can't believe you'd—"

"You should be glad I did! If I hadn't, I never would have found you! Let alone arrived in time to get you out of there!"

"Gloria—" my grandfather ventured, sitting forward slightly.

"And you!" Mrs. Juarez thundered. A pair of incensed brown eyes whirled around in his direction, and my grandfather sat backward so fast his head hit the back of the seat.

"You! Bringing a bunch of children into that place? Children,

Gavin! What were you thinking?" she demanded, then waved her hand in the air before he could answer. "Never mind. I'll deal with you later."

My grandfather gulped.

Mrs. Juarez turned back toward the front.

"Why didn't you tell me?" Sylvie asked quietly. "About Dad. Why didn't you tell me—?"

"That he had become someone I no longer wanted to be married to? Someone I didn't want raising my daughter?"

Sylvie nodded. Mrs. Juarez let out a long sigh.

"Frankly, Sylvie, I was hoping I wouldn't have to tell you. Our divorce is final. It will stay that way, no matter what. I was hoping he would come to his senses about other things. But now I'm not sure that's going to happen."

"It's not," Sylvie said dryly. "Mom, I hardly recognized him in there."

Mrs. Juarez put her hand on top of her daughter's on the center console.

"I'm taking you all back to Central," she said. "Hopefully, once we get there, we'll be able to sort things out."

"And then we can go home, right?" I asked. I felt bad saying it, but if Mr. Juarez really wasn't kidnapped, then we didn't need to be here anymore. I didn't want to think about the lab and the Plutonians and all the things Dr. Marsh had threatened were going to happen. Maybe my grandfather was right—none of it was really our business anyway. I wanted to be back home. Back on Earth. Where my biggest problems were making sure the tennis balls stayed on my spikes and keeping clear of Orlando's pranks.

Mrs. Juarez turned around to look at me. I braced myself for angry-mom face. But instead, her eyes looked soft and sad.

"I don't think it's going to be quite that easy, kiddo," she said. "Some people are waiting for you back at the apartment."

"Me?" I asked. "Why would they be waiting for me?"

"Because you're the Dinosaur Boy!" Chancellor Fontana exclaimed, her face flushed with excitement.

"The what?" I asked, staring at her across the Juarezes' coffee table. She and Ms. Helen were sitting on the opposite sofa, facing me. Elliot and Sylvie sat on either side of me. My grandfather and Mrs. Juarez were on the love seat nearby, and Venetio was perched on the arm of a chair across from them.

"The Dinosaur Boy," she repeated. "You're the talk of Mars!"

"What?" was all I could say in reply.

Chancellor Fontana gestured to Ms. Helen, who dumped an armload of magazines onto the table. They looked like the kind of Earth magazines you see in grocery store checkout lines. Except that these all had Martians on the front.

Well, Martians and me. Every magazine had at least one bad, grainy photo of me on it.

Elliot leaned forward and picked up one that had a close-up of my tail on the cover.

"I thought Sylvie was the famous one," he said.

"Oh, she is. At first, Sawyer was just a faceless member of Sylvie's entourage. You know, like the rest of you," Ms. Helen explained, causing Sylvie to scowl and Elliot to stiffen. "But you know how people are. They're always eager to find the next new thing. And right now, that's Sawyer."

She gestured to the magazines.

I shifted through the pile, cringing at the headlines. They were all in Martian, of course, but the English subtitles were worryingly clear:

Who Is Mars's New "Stego-Cutie"?
ALL THE DETAILS

You Thought Earthlings Were Boring?
Check This One Out!

Get the Look: Plates and Spikes!

What Kind of Dinosaur Would You Be?
Take the Quiz!

There *had* been people yelling "Dino Boy" during our tour of Central. My teeth started to involuntarily grind at this, especially once I saw another magazine that claimed it had obtained "An Exclusive Interview with a Member of the Dinosaur Boy's Inner Circle."

A member of my "inner circle"? Who would—?

I looked accusingly at Venetio, who gave me an embarrassed smile.

"They, um, offered to upgrade my seat," he said sheepishly. "I'm just two rows back from the Kuiper Kickers bench now!"

"Anyhow," Chancellor Fontana said, pulling my attention away from the Plutonian and the magazines, "we're here to ask you something important. We want you to be the next chancellor in charge of the summit."

"What?" I exclaimed. I seemed to be saying that a lot lately. "What happened to the last guy?"

"Actually, the last 'guy' was a lady," Ms. Helen said, squirming slightly in her seat. "Chancellor Gale took over for Chancellor Gio after he grew his second head. And she's just fine. We were able to get her to Central Aquarium before she dried out—"

"The aquarium?" my grandfather asked.

"She was gened. We're pretty sure it was dolphin DNA," Chancellor Fontana explained. "This afternoon, right in the middle of a planning committee meeting, she developed a tail, a back fin, and..." She hesitated.

"And a blowhole," she finished reluctantly. "Right on the top of her head."

"Ew." Sylvie and Elliot shuddered in unison.

"For the moment, Chancellor Gale is only capable of making high-pitched squeal sounds. But she has managed to communicate her desire to resign her position. At least, we're pretty sure that's what she meant to say..." Ms. Helen added thoughtfully.

"Why would you want me to be chancellor?" I asked them both. "I'm a kid. And an Earthling."

"Not just any kid. You're the Dinosaur Boy," Chancellor Fontana corrected me. "You are well-known. Popular. And most importantly you are already...well, you've already got...that is to say, you're not fully—"

"Are you alluding to the fact that my grandson is already a

hybrid and therefore less likely to be a target for gene-ing?" my grandfather interrupted.

"Well...yes," Chancellor Fontana admitted.

"No," my grandfather said darkly. "No, absolutely not. I won't permit it."

"It's just a figurehead position, Dr. Franklin," Ms. Helen said. "The game and the summit are in less than twelve hours. There's no way the BURPSers will have time to get to him in that amount of time."

"And Sawyer is perfect for the job!" added Chancellor Fontana. "He's known, he's liked, and as an Earthling, he's neutral. All of the previous Chancellors were Martians. We believe the Plutonians— even the BURPSers—might accept Sawyer as an impartial facilitator of the vote."

"Might? Might accept him?" my grandfather snapped, shaking his head. "No, I will not allow you to put my grandson at such risk. I'm an Earthling as well. And a hybrid. I'll do it."

"With all due respect, Dr. Franklin," Chancellor Fontana said gently, "no one on this planet knows who you are. We're not asking you. We're asking Sawyer. What do you say, young man?"

I swallowed.

"What would I have to do exactly?" I asked. "As...chancellor?"

"Your first job would be to officially start the game clock at the Friendship and Goodwill Game tomorrow morning," Ms. Helen said. "You'll watch the game from a lovely private box. The nicest in the entire arena."

"A private box?" Venetio piped up.

"Of course you could invite your entourage," Ms. Helen added, gesturing to Venetio and to everybody sitting around me. "The members of the council will also be present. At the conclusion of the game, you'll preside over the vote. The actual summit will take place right there at the arena."

"Speaking of the council," my grandfather asked. "Where is everybody? There seem to be far fewer people here than the last time you came calling."

"Most of them went into hiding," Ms. Helen admitted. "They're afraid of getting gened."

"Then who exactly is running Mars at the moment?" my grandfather persisted.

Chancellor Fontana and Ms. Helen looked at each other.

"That would be us," Chancellor Fontana answered.

"A Plutonian and a Martian who took office two weeks ago?" My grandfather shook his head. "No wonder this is the best plan you can come up with. The answer is no."

"As we said before, Dr. Franklin," Ms. Helen said icily, "we are not asking you. We are asking Sawyer."

She turned to me.

"Well?"

I had no idea what to say. I opened my mouth, hoping that the right answer would come out. But instead, my stomach growled so loudly that everybody in the room jumped.

Mrs. Juarez patted my grandfather's hand—wait a sec, had they been holding hands?—and stood up.

"He'll think about," she announced. "In the meantime, it's time we all had dinner."

◆◆◆

Somehow, between arriving in Mars Central and rescuing us at the lab, Mrs. Juarez had managed to go grocery shopping. And unlike my grandfather, she knew where to find veggies in Mars. I could see several heads of lettuce, as well as some carrots, cucumbers, and radishes sticking out of the reusable grocery bags that were piled in the entryway.

My stomach growled even louder.

Mrs. Juarez stood over the bags, hands on her hips, and started issuing orders like an air traffic controller.

"Gavin and I will brief Ms. Tombaugh and Chancellor Fontana on the lab and the whereabouts of my ex-husband," she said. "Sawyer, Elliot, and Venetio, why don't you bring the bags into the kitchen and start unloading? Sylvie, you can start the dough for the empanadas. I'll come and join you in a moment."

Elliot, Venetio, and I rushed to obey. But Sylvie made no move toward the kitchen.

"Why do I have to start the food?" she asked dangerously. "Because I'm a girl?"

Mrs. Juarez snorted, like these were the last words she expected to hear out of her daughter's mouth.

"I'm not sure what being a girl has to do with it, *mi hija*. More the fact that I taught you how to make empanadas before you knew how to walk. But if you don't think you can handle it on your own, you're welcome to wait until I'm through here—"

"No," Sylvie snapped. "I've got it."

"You're sure? Because if you've forgotten how to do it—"

"I said I've got it." Sylvie flopped her arms up in exasperation and disappeared into the kitchen.

Mrs. Juarez turned to me, an amused look on her face.

"Sometimes you just have to know what buttons to push," she said with a wink.

Our meal of black bean and banana empanadas (for them) and a huge salad of fresh greens (for me) tasted like heaven after all of those Nutri Nuggets. With my stomach full, I had no trouble drifting off to sleep. In spite of all the weird stuff on my mind.

When I woke up sometime later in the middle of the night, I had to remind myself where I was.

Mars. Where they want me to be the chancellor of the vote to kick the Plutonians out of the Intergalactic Soccer Federation.

That sentence definitely wouldn't have made any sense to me last week.

I looked over to the other side of the guest bed, expecting to see Elliot passed out and snoring. But instead, there was just a crumpled blanket and a dent in the pillow where his head had been.

Elliot was gone.

The Thing about Elliot...

I didn't have to go far to find him. Elliot was in the living room. Alone. Doing soccer drills with a single-minded determination that could only mean he was upset about something.

"Elliot?" I asked.

"Busy!" he called, running in place and tapping first one foot, then the other on top of a stationary soccer ball.

"Doing what?"

"Practicing!"

"It's the middle of the night," I pointed out. "Why are you practicing now?"

"Because."

"Because why?"

"Because that triceratops scientist guy was right!"

"Huh?"

Elliot paused to wipe a streak of sweat off his forehead.

"I am a basic, run-of-the-mill, thoroughly uninteresting human," he said and then abruptly turned his back, dribbling the ball toward the couch and away from me.

"That's ridiculous!" I said.

"Is it?" Elliot asked over one shoulder. "I'm not a hybrid, like you and Sylvie and your grandfather. I'm not blue like Venetio. I'm just an Earthling. There's nothing special about me."

"Sure there is!" I said.

"Oh yeah? Name one thing!"

"Basketball!" I exclaimed. Which may have been sort of a weird thing to say when he was playing around with a soccer ball, but it was true. Basketball was Elliot's thing. He'd been wearing his University of Oregon Ducks jersey for the past three days. Not that either of us had brought a change of clothes with us to Mars, but still...

"Ha!" he scoffed over his shoulder.

"I'm serious!" I said, leaning against one side of the couch. "You're the best basketball player I know! You're going to be the star of that traveling team this summer. Everybody says so."

He stopped, letting the soccer ball roll away from him. When he finally spoke, his voice was so quiet I could barely hear him. "I didn't make it."

"Didn't make what?" I asked.

"The team. The traveling team. I tried out, but I didn't make it. They said no."

"Oh."

"Turns out, there's more to basketball than just being tall."

"Oh," I said again.

I didn't know what else to say. No wonder Elliot had been quiet lately. Ever since his growth spurt, basketball had been the only thing that made him feel normal. What would he do without that?

We stood in silence for a good minute or two. Finally, Elliot asked, "What am I doing here, Sawyer?"

I spread my hands.

"What are any of us doing here, Elliot? It's Mars! It would be weird if we didn't feel out of place."

"But everybody else seems to have a reason for being here. Sylvie came to find her dad. Your grandfather is helping her. And he needed to bring you along to get us into the lab. And look at you! You've been here like five minutes and you're already famous. They want you to be chancellor! While I'm still just… What did Ms. Helen call me? 'A faceless member of Sylvie's entourage.' Or maybe your entourage now, I don't know. I think I'm always going to be that. Faceless. Un-special."

"Of course you're not," I told him.

He shrugged and then looked down at the soccer ball.

"Maybe I just need a new thing. Venetio says I'd make a good soccer goalie. Maybe if I practice enough—"

"Elliot, that's not going to—"

"What do you know?" he demanded, starting to get angry now. "You don't get it! You're one of them now. You're famous!"

"I'm not—" I began. But then I remembered the magazine articles, and I stopped.

"What are you guys doing out here?"

Sylvie walked through the doorway, wearing pink plaid pajamas and a frown.

Elliot threw his hands up into the air.

"Oh perfect," he said to the ceiling. "Another one."

"Another one what?" Sylvie asked, crossing her arms defensively and leaning against an armchair.

"Another 'special' person," Elliot sneered. "I'm surrounded by extra-special people."

Sylvie raised an eyebrow at me. I shrugged, not really sure how to explain.

She pointed a finger at Elliot.

"You don't know everything about me, Elliot," she said warningly. "Don't pretend that you do!"

"And whose fault is that?" Elliot demanded, staring her down. "You don't tell anybody anything. I'm more mad at you than at anybody else."

"At me?" Sylvie put her hands on her hips. "Why me?"

"Because! This whole thing with the Plutonians is your fault!"

"*My* fault?" Sylvie repeated, looking questioningly at me.

"Yes!" Elliot yelled. "Yours and every other stupid Martian on this planet!"

"What?" Sylvie exclaimed.

"Why do you hate the Plutonians so much?" he asked. "There's nothing wrong with them. Why go to all this trouble to keep them out of the ISF?"

"Because of the BURPSers, you idiot!" Sylvie spat at him. "They're dangerous! You heard what Dr. Marsh said they were planning to do—"

"The BURPSers didn't exist until the Martians got everyone to officially declare that Pluto isn't a planet anymore. Why'd you have to do that? Why couldn't you have just left them alone?"

Sylvie opened her mouth to reply and then closed it again.

"There isn't even a good reason for it, is there?" Elliot asked. "It was just mean. And the whole summit thing? The Friendship and Goodwill Game? It's bologna. It's just a show they're putting on to make people think the vote is fair. But it isn't. Everybody knows how it's going to go. The Martian Council has already decided."

"So what?" Sylvie hissed. "Even if that's true, what should we do? Let the BURPSers take over Mars? Let them gene all of the Martians?"

"Maybe we should!" Elliot spat back at her. "Maybe the Martians should find out what it feels like to be one of us un-special ones for a change!"

"You can't possibly mean—" Sylvie started, but I cut her off.

"I have a plan," I said. I did. Sort of. A strange, half-baked inkling of a plan, which Elliot's words had just added some fuel to. "I think there's a way we can save the Martians *and* the Plutonians. If we—"

"Just like we saved all of those bullies at our school from the Jupiterians?" Elliot scoffed. "Great. You guys go knock yourselves out. But I, for one, am totally sick of saving the bad guy. So you're just going to have to do this one without me."

He spun around on his heel and marched into our room, leaving Sylvie and me alone in the living room.

Sylvie's lower lip was quivering.

"Are you OK?" I asked hesitantly. "He shouldn't have said those things. Not after everything that happened with your dad—"

"I'm fine." Sylvie sniffed, and wiped her nose with the sleeve of her pajamas. She marched off toward her bedroom, pausing only to step over Venetio, who was asleep in his pile of blankets in front of her door.

I found my grandfather in the kitchen. Eating the remains of the giant salad Mrs. Juarez had made me for dinner.

Without a word, he passed me a fork. We chewed in silence for a couple of minutes.

"Can I ask you something?" I said finally.

"Shoot," he said, spearing a piece of cucumber.

"The Star Wars plan," I said and then hesitated about how to phrase the question. "Did you bring me on this trip just to use me?" I asked finally.

"Use you?" he asked, his mouth full.

"Yeah. You know, because of my dinosaur parts. Was I just an excuse to get us into the lab?"

My grandfather swallowed.

"Sawyer, I brought you on this trip because you are a brave, resourceful, and smart kid. I knew finding Sylvie's dad was going to be tough. And when I thought about who could help me do it, you immediately came to mind. I didn't think up the Star Wars thing until after we got here."

"Oh," I said, feeling a bit foolish.

"Why would you ask me that?"

I shrugged. "I don't know. Elliot was saying something to me about everybody having a purpose here. And I guess I don't really understand yours. Why do you care so much about finding Sylvie's dad?"

My grandfather rubbed the back of his neck like it was sore or something.

"Well, partly because she's your friend and she was worried about him. And partly because...well, because of Gloria," he stammered, turning a bit red.

They had been holding hands! I knew it!

"Oh. So you and Sylvie's mom..." I didn't know quite what to say to that.

"We didn't want to tell you and Sylvie until we were sure it was serious."

"Is it serious?" I asked hesitantly. "I mean, do you, like, love her and stuff?"

"I do," my grandfather said. And his eyes went all soft, sort of gooey. I had never seen him look like that before. "She was worried about her ex-husband. I thought if I could find him, I could put her mind at ease. I thought it would be something I could do for her. Before..."

He trailed off, then paused to stretch the back of his neck.

"Enough about me," he said finally. "What about you? Have you given any more thought to the chancellor thing?"

"I know you don't want me to do it," I said quickly.

He grimaced, still rubbing his neck.

"I know you keep saying this isn't our problem, that we shouldn't get involved," I added. "But I've been thinking... Maybe it should be our problem."

He groaned.

"No, seriously," I went on. "I mean, what will happen to the Plutonians if they're never anybody's problem? And what about the Martians who are going to get gened? Maybe I'm the only one impartial enough to—"

My grandfather groaned again, and I was beginning to think it didn't have anything to do with what I was saying.

"Are you OK?" I asked, standing up in alarm.

"I'm fine," my grandfather said, but I could tell he wasn't. He was breathing hard and when he stood up, he had to hold on to the edge of the table. "I just—"

He groaned again and leaned forward over the table.

"My jacket," he said, his voice tight. "Help me get it off!"

I rushed around behind him and helped him ease one arm, and then the other, out of his sleeves. But it wasn't until I peeled the jacket off his back that I saw why he was in so much pain.

There were holes in the back of the white, button-down shirt he was wearing underneath. Two long rows of them. And each hole had a tiny, stegosaurus plate peeking through it.

Cure, Shmure

The jacket fell from my hands and made a leather puddle on the kitchen floor.

"But—the cure! You took the cure!" I stammered.

My grandfather sighed in relief and sank back down into his chair, only to jump up again a second later, grabbing his backside.

His tail, I realized. His tail is growing back too!

"The cure stopped working a couple of weeks ago," he explained, bracing his elbows on the table and lowering himself gently so that only one side of his bottom rested on the very edge of the chair. "At least I suspected that's what was happening. I had the symptoms: pain, hunger. But my blood tests were inconclusive. I wasn't one hundred percent sure what was happening until a couple of days ago. When everything started to grow back."

"So the cure doesn't work?" I asked, thinking of the blue vial sitting on top of my bookcase at home. It had been my choice not to take it. I had chosen to stay part dinosaur. But I had always sort of liked the idea that it was there. Just in case. But now...

"Evidently not." My grandfather sighed, still shifting around the chair, trying to find a comfortable position.

"So if the BURPSers gene all of the Martians, like Dr. Marsh said they were going to, he won't be able to turn them back? The cure won't work?"

"No, it won't," my grandfather said, wincing as he accidentally shifted his weight onto his tail stub. "This is what comes of fooling around with things you don't fully understand. I warned Otto this would happen. I tried to tell him what was happening with me—"

"You did! You did start to tell him! Right before I—" I remembered suddenly, then I felt my heart sink. "Right before I triggered the alarm. It's my fault. I didn't let you finish."

My grandfather risked his precarious balance to put a hand on my arm.

"He wouldn't have believed me anyway," he told me. "You heard him. He's too far gone. Too obsessed with his own genius to admit failure or even a fault. It wouldn't have mattered if I had told him everything."

"What about the Martian police?" I persisted. "You told Ms. Helen and Chancellor Fontana where the lab is, right? Couldn't they—"

"I spoke to Ms. Helen when we returned to the apartment, and again just a few moments ago. The Martian police found the lab, but the scientists and Sylvie's father had already sealed themselves inside. Ms. Helen thinks it'll be at least twenty-four hours before the Martians can blast their way in. By then—"

"The summit will be over," I finished heavily.

My grandfather nodded.

"Which says to me that Dr. Marsh has already done his part and is just biding his time. Whatever he and the BURPSers are planning, I'll bet it happens soon. We have to think of a way to keep the Martians from kicking the Plutonians out of the ISF tomorrow."

I stared down at the table. Somebody had to do something. But did it really have to be me?

"Hey," I said, thinking of something else. "When you said you wanted to do something for Sylvie's mom 'before.' Did you mean before all of your dinosaur parts came back?" I asked.

My grandfather sighed heavily.

"I've been down this road before, Sawyer. With your grandmother."

"My grandmother?" I repeated. I tried to think if he had ever mentioned her before. My mother only brought her up occasionally. And never in a particularly nice way.

"Yes. She was a paleontologist, of all things, so she understood more than most what was happening to me. She was supportive at first. But eventually, she decided she didn't want to be married to a part-dinosaur. What if Gloria—"

"What if Gloria what?"

Mrs. Juarez was standing in the doorway. From there, she had a perfect view of my grandfather's back. And his two rows of budding plates.

My grandfather's head snapped up at the sound of her voice. I could see the muscles in his arms tighten, like he was thinking about jumping up or turning around or doing something to hide what was happening to him. But instead, he stayed perfectly still and stared blankly at the tabletop.

"Oh," Mrs. Juarez said quietly. "Oh my…"

"I'd better get some sleep," I said, getting up from my chair as quickly as I could and leaving the two of them alone in the kitchen.

No Thanks on That Hamster DNA

It was very late, but I wasn't feeling particularly tired. I couldn't think of anything useful to do, so I eventually wandered into the hall bathroom, thinking I might brush my teeth.

I clicked on the light and froze.

Venetio was there. One of his blue hands was clutching an open vial of cloudy liquid.

The other was holding my toothbrush.

Neither of us moved or spoke for at least a full minute.

Finally, Venetio cleared his throat.

"They asked you to be the new chancellor," he said.

"That's right," I said slowly.

"That means I'm supposed to infect you with this"—he nodded to the vial—"for Pluto. But I-I don't…"

"You don't want to," I finished for him.

He shook his head miserably.

"No, I don't want to."

"What is it?" I asked, honestly curious.

He shrugged. "A serum. Some kind of rodent gene," he said. "Hamster or something. I didn't ask. I didn't really want to know."

I nodded and gave a small sigh of relief that I had avoided becoming the first-ever stegosaurus–human–hamster hybrid. At least for the moment.

"So," I said, trying to sound casual. "You didn't really win your ticket from a radio station, did you?"

Venetio shook his head.

"No! I mean, yes, I won the ticket. But I didn't have any way to get to Mars. The ship I borrowed didn't really belong to my mom—it belonged to the BURPSers. I'm not one of them—I didn't lie to you about that. But I guess you could say I'm working for them. Kind of."

"Kind of?"

"Well, I wasn't really supposed to have to do anything. They put me in an old busted ship and dropped me off right next to yours. The same way they stuck stowaways on every ship headed to Mars that they could. Just in case. They gave me this…this serum stuff and said there was a tiny chance I might have to use it on somebody. But I never thought I'd actually have to go through with it. I mean, how was I supposed to know they'd nominate a dinosaur kid to be chancellor?"

"I see your point," I said. I did. Sort of.

"Plus, they told me they had a cure for the gene-ing," Venetio added. "That they could reverse it. So I figured, what was the harm? I would get to go to the game. And on the small chance I ended up having to gene somebody, it could be undone. No harm, no foul. But now—" He hesitated.

"You heard everything my grandfather and I were talking about?" I asked.

Venetio nodded.

"I can't do it," he said. "Not now that I know you. And not now that I know they can't undo it."

"Um…thank you?" I mumbled, not really knowing what else to say.

"But I also can't let them vote to ban the Plutonians from the ISF," he added, looking quite conflicted. "I can't do that either."

"Why?" I asked him. "I mean, I know you like soccer, Venetio, but why do you care so much about this? Enough to almost gene me?"

"Well, for one thing, my mom works for the ISF," Venetio explained, putting my toothbrush back on the counter. "If Pluto gets kicked out, she'll lose her job. Things aren't great on Pluto right now. Who knows when she'll be able to find a new one?"

"Oh."

"Plus, if they do this, who knows what they'll do next? Mars hates us. And all the other planets always follow their lead. If Mars decides they don't want to trade with us anymore or let us visit their planet anymore, the other planets will decide the same thing. Mars isn't going to stop until Pluto, and all the Plutonians, are all alone. Way out on our icy little rock with nowhere else to go."

"Oh," I said again, and for some reason, all I could picture was Orlando sitting by himself at that big, empty table in the cafeteria.

"I know it's wrong for the BURPSers to go around gene-ing people," he continued. "But it's also wrong for the Martians to treat us this way, just because they don't like us. Everybody's wrong. How am I supposed to pick a side when everybody is wrong?"

I took a deep breath.

"Maybe we need to make our own side," I suggested.

"Sure," Venetio scoffed.

"I'm serious! Listen, I know you were passed out when Dr. Marsh told us everything. But do you know the BURPSers are planning to gene all of the Martians?"

He nodded.

"Maybe some of them deserve it," I allowed. "But most don't. And maybe the BURPSers deserve to be punished, but not every Plutonian does. There are way more good Martians than bad ones, and way more good Plutonians than BURPSers. But nobody's fighting for them. Maybe it's time someone did."

"Like us?" Venetio asked, sounding doubtful.

"Yes," I said, suddenly feeling way more sure of myself than I had in a long time. "The BURPSers cooked up this whole plan with Sunder Labs because they were assuming that the Martian Council was going to vote to ban the Plutonians from the ISF. But what if I make sure that doesn't happen?"

"How are you going to do that?" Venetio asked.

"I'm going to be chancellor, that's how," I said. "After the game tomorrow, I think I can get the Martian Council to change their minds. If I can do that, then maybe the BURPSers will back down. Maybe—"

Venetio shook his head slowly.

"They're not going to wait for the vote. It's the game, Sawyer. It's all about the game."

◆◆◆

"It's simple, really," Venetio said after I had gathered my grandfather, Mrs. Juarez, and Sylvie in the living room. Elliot had not responded to my knock on the door—he probably was still mad at me. "If they want to avoid getting gened, the Martians have to win the soccer game tomorrow."

"I don't get it," my grandfather said, and I was glad I wasn't the only one. "What does the soccer game have to do with the entire planet getting gened?"

"The BURPSers are planning to gene the Martian water supply, sir," Venetio explained. "There are a dozen BURPSers disguised as Kuiper Kicker fans on the planet right now, just waiting to do it. But they have a problem."

He held up his wrist with the metal tracking bracelet.

"Every Plutonian in Mars is wearing one of these. The BURPSers have to get away from their escorts to do the gene-ing, but if all of them just suddenly run out of wristband range, the alarms will go off and the police will be on them in a second. They need a distraction. Something that the police will be even more worried about than them."

"Like the soccer game," I said.

Venetio nodded, but Sylvie was shaking her head.

"If the game is just a distraction, then why does it matter who wins?"

"Because the first phase of the gene-ing is going to take place during the toast," Venetio said.

"The toast at the end of the game?" I asked. "The one the losers have to make to the winners?"

Venetio nodded.

"Each team plans a drink for the toast, just in case they win. The Martians are planning to use Nutri Juice," he reminded us. "I don't know what the Plutonians brought, but the BURPSers added a little something extra to it. The losers have to drink whatever the winners pour for them. If the Plutonians win, the entire Martian team will get gened. With Plutonian DNA."

"Right there in the stadium?" Sylvie asked, her eyes wide with shock. "In front of everyone? People are going to flip out."

"That's the idea," Venetio said, looking a tad embarrassed. "If there's chaos in the stadium, the Martian police will be too busy dealing with it to notice the BURPSers sneaking off. By the time they calm everybody down, it'll be too late. The water will be gened. And anybody who drinks it will be gened too."

"That'll be everybody," my grandfather muttered. "The whole planet. Just like Otto said."

"Geez," I muttered, picturing an entire planet of newly blue, confused Martian-Plutonians.

Sylvie was glaring at Venetio.

"You knew about this? And you're just telling us now? When it's too late to do anything about it?"

Venetio wrung his hands. "Look, I know it sounds bad. I do. But Sunder Labs told the BURPSers they had a cure. Nobody thought this was going to be permanent."

"But now we know the cure doesn't work," Mrs. Juarez said, absentmindedly touching one of my grandfather's growing plates.

Venetio nodded. "That's why the Martians have to win tomorrow, ma'am. If they win, they won't have to drink the Plutonian toast. And the BURPSers won't get the distraction they need to gene everybody else."

"Why risk letting them play at all?" I asked. "Why don't we just call off the game? We could just tell Chancellor Fontana and—"

"No way," Sylvia said, looking at Venetio. "Remember when they tried to cancel the '09 Finals, because of a sandstorm on Jupiter? There were riots."

"So?" I asked. "I mean, riots aren't great, but wouldn't that be better than everybody in Mars getting gened?"

"No, Sylvie's right," my grandfather put in. "If the BURPSers are looking for a distraction, a riot would be a good one. Maybe even better than waiting until the end of the game. If a stadium full of people are suddenly running around like crazy, the police would never notice a dozen BURPSers leaving their escorts."

"There were riots after the '14 Finals too," Mrs. Juarez said thoughtfully. "When the Martians won on penalty kicks after Tycho Brawn got fouled—"

"Took a dive," Venetio corrected her.

"Whatever," Mrs. Juarez continued, just as Sylvie opened her mouth. "My point is, a questionable call could cause a riot too. If the Martians win on penalty kicks again or in some other contro-versial way—"

"Like sudden death," Venetio interrupted. "The Plutonians hate that rule. If the Martians win during sudden death, there will be a riot for sure. Plutonians are convinced the Martians have figured out a way to rig it."

"That's ridiculous!" Sylvie protested. "Sudden death is random. It's programmed into the game clock!"

"OK." I cut in before Venetio could respond. "So the Martians have to win in a totally clean, non-sketchy way. But the main thing is, they have to win. How can we make sure that happens?"

Venetio, my grandfather, Mrs. Juarez, and I all looked at Sylvie. She shook her head.

"Nope."

"Sylvie—" I began.

"It's not like they need me anyway," she retorted. "There's no way Mars is going to lose tomorrow. Tycho Brawn even came out of retirement to play!"

"If that's true," my grandfather said, "then the BURPSers will have planned for that. Wouldn't it make sense for them to have a backup, some sort of insurance, to make sure the game goes their way?"

We all looked at Venetio, who spread his hands.

"If they do, I haven't heard about it. I'm just a sleeper cell, remem-ber? It's not like they told me everything."

"What about the vote?" I asked. "Does the vote matter at all?"

"It matters," Venetio assured me. "If the Martians vote to ban

Pluto from the ISF, a lot of Plutonians will be upset. And a lot more of them might start listening to the BURPSers."

"So it sounds like we need to do two things," my grandfather summed up. "We need to secure an uncontroversial Martian victory in the game tomorrow, and we need to get the Council to vote against the Plutonian ban."

"I have an idea about the vote," I said. My inkling had grown leaps and bounds in the last hour.

"And the game?" Venetio asked, giving Sylvie a hard look. "If she won't play, then we're going to have to make sure the Martians win some other way—a way that won't cause riots."

"How are we going to do that?" Mrs. Juarez asked, looking at me. They were all looking at me.

I sighed.

"I have no idea."

The room that Elliot and I shared was dark. There was just enough light coming in through the enormous windows for me to see a long lump stretched out on Elliot's side of the bed.

"Elliot," I said without turning the lights on. "I really need to talk to you."

The lump was silent.

"Look, I know we're fighting. I know you're mad. But you're my best friend. And there's a lot of stuff going on right now."

The lump did not respond.

I sighed.

"Please, Elliot. You don't have to stop being mad at me. You don't even have to talk if you don't want to. But will you listen to me? Just for a minute?"

The lump still didn't say anything. And now I was starting to get mad.

"Elliot. Come on!"

I flipped on the light.

He wasn't there. The lump was just a twisted mess of covers. But there was a folded-up piece of paper on my pillow. It said:

I officially resign from your entourage.

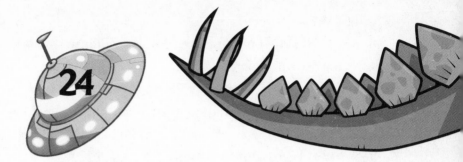

We, Who Are about to Dive…

Welcome to the 2016 Summit Friendship and Goodwill Game!"

The deep, booming voice was at odds with the tiny-even-for-a-Martian Martian who sat behind the microphone. He was in a see-through booth that adjoined what Chancellor Fontana assured us was the largest private box in the arena.

Even from behind the box's thick glass window, I could hear the cheering outside. The stadium was packed. And from up here, the crowd looked like a red-and-blue splatter painting. There were no Home or Visitor sections. There couldn't be, since all the Plutonians had to stay within ten meters of their Martian escorts.

Every Plutonian except Venetio, that is. His wrist cuff had been deactivated that morning (by Chancellor Fontana). But nobody else knew that. Not even Sylvie, who sat glumly beside him in the seats closest to the window. My grandfather was there as well, sitting off to the side and sweating heavily underneath a large trench coat. His plates had grown larger overnight. The cure was wearing off even faster now. I had tried to convince him to stay home and take care of himself, but he had refused.

The only person missing was Elliot. He hadn't come back to the apartment that morning. Not knowing where he was felt like someone was punching me in the stomach. Repeatedly. But there was nothing I could do about him right now.

I had a planet to save. Two, in fact. And Elliot had made it clear that he didn't want any part of it.

"Please give a big Martian welcome to your very own Red Razers!"

The cheering outside intensified. I didn't even have to look down to see the line of red-jerseyed Razers run onto the field behind Coach Kepler. I had a perfect view of them on the Jumbotron immediately across the stadium from the box.

"And please welcome our distinguished visitors, the Kuiper Kickers from the dwarf planet of Pluto!"

"Dwarf planet. I guess he couldn't resist throwing that in," Venetio said, groaning. Outside, a mixture of cheers and boos erupted through the crowd as a line of blue-jerseyed Plutonians trotted onto the field.

Ms. Helen threw the announcer a miffed look. He shrugged and spread his hands in a *What?* gesture, then pointed to me.

"And now the moment you've all been waiting for…"

Ms. Helen handed me a microphone, and Chancellor Fontana shoved me in front of a banner that read **Nutri Nuggets: Proud Sponsor of the Red Razers. Fear the Red!**

Before I could protest that this was hardly proclaiming my

neutrality, a Martian with a headset pointed a camera at me and suddenly my face appeared on the Jumbotron.

"You know him as the Dinosaur Boy! Visiting us all the way from Earth, please welcome our newest summit chancellor, Sawyer Bronson!"

There was a round of applause from outside, far less then for either of the two soccer teams. I couldn't stop staring at my giant face on the screen. I looked like I was about to be sick.

"Sawyer!" Ms. Helen hissed, then pointed frantically to a teleprompter, which was typing out words just underneath the camera lens.

"Uh, welcome?" I said.

It came out squeaky, so I cleared my throat and tried again.

"Welcome!"

Ms. Helen jumped behind the camera and smiled a grossly exaggerated ear-to-ear grin. I tried to copy her, but the part-dinosaur on the Jumbotron still looked pretty nauseous. I couldn't help it. All fifty thousand people in the stadium were staring at me. The very thought made me want to spew my breakfast salad all over the camera lens.

I tried to ignore my stomach and concentrate on the words Chancellor Fontana and Ms. Helen had written out for me that morning.

"On behalf of the Martian Council, I'd like to welcome you to this very special Friendship and Goodwill Game. I see today not as a rivalry between two teams, but as a coming together of two extraordinary groups of people. I am confident that the friendship and camaraderie we have cultivated in the past weeks will remain alive and well, regardless of the outcome of today's game. Or of today's vote."

I squinted over to the other side of the box, where the twelve members of the Martian Council all sat together at a long table. With the exception of Chancellor Fontana, they had all come out of hiding just that morning. And most of them still looked a little shocked to be out and about.

Ms. Helen started motioning for me to wrap it up.

"So, let's have a clean and fair match!" I finished, with a pointed look at Chancellor Fontana. It had been her job to "strongly advise" Coach Kepler to avoid any controversial plays. The Martian players didn't know about the BURPSers' plan, but they had wholeheartedly agreed to do what they could to avoid any rioting.

One of the camera Martian's assistants began to pull on a large crank. The front window opened, just enough for me to stick my arm out. I couldn't even lean my head out to see what I was doing. Luckily, one of the outside cameras was still broadcasting me on the Jumbotron, so I was able to use that to see where the red button on the top of the game clock was.

I pressed down on the button, and the clock gave a sharp click.

"*Let the game begin!*"

I've seen soccer games on TV before, and honestly, the Martian-Plutonian game wasn't that much different.

Aside from the fact that half of the players were blue and the other half had antennae.

There was a lot of running back and forth. A lot of pushing and shoving, some of which was apparently legal and some not. The referees—one Martian, one Plutonian—gave out handfuls of cards for various violations. One time, the refs themselves nearly came to blows over whether a Martian player had intentionally tripped a Plutonian. The two coaches had to break them apart and each side donated a thirty-second time-out so that the refs could cool off enough to keep going.

"*The Martians are starting their attack again! It's Jakosky, passing to Banerdt. Banerdt to Radha. Radha back to Jakosky, then over to Zubrin. Zubrin to Brawn for the shot…and it's wide. Plutonian ball.*"

During the times when an attempt on goal did not appear to be imminent, the announcer filled the empty airtime by giving the crowd background on the players.

"*And wearing number forty-two for the Razers is Tycho Brawn. Who, of course, is famous for scoring the winning goal for the Martians in the '14 Finals.*"

"That's him?" I asked Sylvie, leaning toward the window as the outside camera broadcast a live shot of number forty-two trotting down the field. He was bald and bearded. And also quite tall for a Martian; he towered over every other player on the field.

"Yup," Sylvie said without enthusiasm.

"Is there something weird about his nose?" I asked, squinting.

"There was a botched gene-ing attempt a few years ago," Sylvie told us. "Tycho's nose turned into a beak. He had it removed. But the replacement didn't really take. He wears a plastic nose now, but it looks a little bit weird. He doesn't like to talk about it."

"Forget the nose," Venetio said, frowning down at the field. "Does anyone else think he looks sort of…tired?"

Before either Sylvie or I could respond, the announcer's voice boomed through the box again.

"*Tycho Brawn is probably Mars's best hope for a goal today. Let's hope he picks up the pace a little bit!*"

On the field, the bearded Martian giant stopped in mid-stride and rested his elbows on his knees.

"Not just me then," Venetio said.

"That's the great Tycho Brawn?" I asked, incredulous. I could feel my heart sinking. "That's the guy we're counting on to win it for the Martians?"

"*This is definitely not the lightning-fast Brawn we know and love! Come on, Martians. Let's perk him up with a cheer! Fear the Red! Fear the Red! Fear the Red!*"

The Martians in the crowd picked up the chant. Tycho Brawn eventually got it together and rejoined the action, but he stilled looked like he was moving at about half the speed of the other players.

I looked at Sylvie. She shrugged.

"Maybe he's conserving his energy for the second half?" she guessed, sounding doubtful.

"Well, the good news is that the Plutonians aren't looking much better," Venetio pointed out, as one of the players in a blue jersey went to kick the ball, missed, and fell flat on his back in midfield. Muttering quietly under his breath, he added, "I never thought I'd be happy to say that."

"Sylvie," I said urgently. "It's not too late. Are you absolutely sure that you—"

"I told you," she said, her voice getting all growly. "I'm. Not. Playing."

I opened my mouth to argue with her, but I was interrupted when Mrs. Juarez walked into the box holding a large, covered tray.

"Food's here!" she announced gaily.

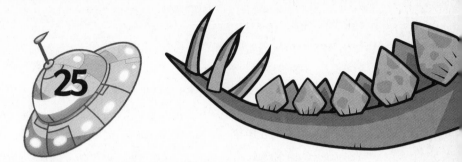

Sudden Death(s)

To the twelve members of the Martian Council (most of whom had been surviving for some time on whatever Nutri Nuggets they could get smuggled to them while in hiding), the smell coming from Mrs. Juarez's tray was irresistible. Some of them were openly salivating. Which was exactly what I had been counting on.

Still, they all had suspicious looks on their faces. None of them made a move to open the steaming foil cylinders that had been placed in front of them.

I stepped up to the table.

"Ladies and gentlemen, I know that the threat of gene-ing is on all of our minds. That's why I had this food prepared especially for us by a celebrity chef from a neutral planet. I believe Gloria Juarez requires no introduction."

There were murmurs of recognition from around the table.

Apparently, Mama Juarez's Mexican-Martian fusion restaurants were as well-known in Mars as Sylvie had claimed.

"Chef Juarez, what exactly have you prepared for us?" asked the elderly Martian at the head of the table as he cautiously unwrapped his foil package. He didn't touch anything inside; he just squinted at it. Even though I could have sworn I saw him lick his lips.

"These are an Earth delicacy called tacos," Mrs. Juarez explained, handing me one as well. "Today I have prepared a breakfast variety for you called migas: a mixture of scrambled eggs, onions, peppers, and tortilla chips, all covered in a melted cheese sauce and wrapped in a flour tortilla. They're very popular in the Tex-Mex cooking tradition."

"Mmmm," I said, unwrapping one end of my taco and taking a healthy bite. It really was good. Not exactly on the regular stegosaurus menu, but still tasty. Mrs. Juarez had somehow even managed to find real Earth chicken eggs.

Not that I wouldn't have choked down a Bruno egg to make my point. But I was glad I didn't have to.

Emboldened by my example, several of the council members took experimental nibbles of their own tacos. Chancellor Fontana took an enormous bite, wiped a drip of sauce off her chin, and grinned.

"It's delicious!" she exclaimed, prompting the remaining holdouts (even the old guy) to tear into their tacos as well.

Mrs. Juarez winked at me, and I breathed a sigh of relief.

Then a heart-stoppingly loud gong sound shook the entire box. Outside, there was a burst of orangey-yellow fire as four walls of flame rose up along the perimeter of the field.

The announcer hurriedly swallowed his bite of taco.

"The first sudden death period has begun!"

What Sylvie had said about knowing you were in sudden death was starting to make sense. It wasn't just the edges of the field that were on fire; the ball was on fire as well.

And so was Tycho Brawn. Metaphorically speaking anyway.

The burly Martian came alive at the sound of the gong. Suddenly he was everywhere at once, tearing around the field so fast he made all the other players look like they were moving in slow motion.

"Finally!" the announcer was shrieking as Brawn charged down the field, kicking the flaming ball ahead of him and heading straight for the Plutonian goal. *"Tycho Brawn has come back to life! He can win it for the Martians right now!"*

"No!" Venetio shouted. He and Sylvie both leaped to their feet. "If the Martians win in sudden death—"

I turned and put a finger to my lips, nodding toward the twelve munching members of the council behind me. Venetio shut up, but we all held our breath as Tycho Brawn easily dodged a Plutonian defender and then launched a lightning-fast shot at the goal.

The Plutonian goalie caught the ball, but barely, just as the fire sputtered out around the field and the first sudden death period came to an end.

There was a collective groan from the Martians in the stands and matching disappointed sounds from the twelve Martians sitting around the table. All of which covered up the four frantic sighs of relief that came from me, Sylvie, Venetio, and Mrs. Juarez.

There was also a painful-sounding grunt from my grandfather, who was still huddled beneath his coat in the corner, an untouched taco beside him.

"Injury time-out!" the announcer said, his mouth full of taco. *"It looks as though Stern—the Plutonian goalie—is on fire! Repeat: Stern is on fire!"*

On the field, a knot of blue-jerseyed players surrounded the Plutonian goalie, who was rolling around on the grass, trying to put himself out.

With a worried look at the lump in the corner that was my grandfather, I sat down beside Sylvie and Venetio. They were already in deep, whispered conversation.

"Chancellor Fontana warned the Martian team not to do anything controversial," Venetio pointed out. "Why would Tycho Brawn only start to play hard during sudden death?"

Sylvie shook her head.

"I don't know."

"That's exactly what the BURPSers would want him to do," Venetio pointed out. "He must be working for them."

"But he's a Martian hero," I reminded him. "He wouldn't do that. Would he, Sylvie?"

Sylvie was staring out of the window.

"Sylvie?" I repeated.

"He took a dive," she muttered, so quietly I could barely hear her.

"What?" Venetio asked, moving his ear closer.

"He dove, OK?" she said in a loud, furious whisper. "In the '14 Finals. He didn't get fouled. He faked it."

"Are you sure?" I asked, as my brain struggled to figure out how this applied to our current situation.

"Yes. Coach Kepler told him to fake a foul so we'd get penalty kicks and win the game."

"How do you know?" I asked.

"Because Kepler asked me to dive first, and I wouldn't do it. So he asked Tycho instead."

"And do you think he's doing it again now?" I asked. "Only trying to score during sudden death to cause a riot for the BURPSers? Why would he do that? He's a Martian! He loves Mars!"

"Tycho loves money," Sylvie growled. "After the '14 Finals, the Martian Council paid him. Very well. If the BURPSers offered him money to throw the game their way, I'll bet he took it."

"He's their insurance policy," Venetio muttered. "Your grandfather was right. The BURPSers are going to make sure this game goes their way."

Down on the field, the injured Plutonian goalie was being hauled off on a stretcher.

"*As regular time resumes, the Plutonians are going to have to substitute in a new goalkeeper.*"

A fresh Plutonian jogged onto the field and took his place in front of the Plutonian goal.

"My, he's a tall one, isn't he, ladies and gentlemen? Has he—yes! I just received word that he cleared the DNA check. He is definitely at least fifty-one percent Plutonian."

I took a closer look at the lanky figure in the Plutonian goal, and I felt my heart drop to my feet.

"Ladies and gentlemen, please welcome, in his debut soccer match, number eighty-four for the Kuiper Kickers, Elliot Foster!"

Sylvie and I stared at each other. I have no idea what my face looked like at that moment, but hers was equal parts horror and disbelief.

"How is that possible?" I asked. "He's not a Plutonian!"

"They said he passed the DNA test," Venetio said slowly.

Sylvie gasped as a bigger-than-life image of Elliot appeared on the Jumbotron.

"He looks…" she started, and then gasped again. "Is he…just a little bit…?"

"Blue," I finished grimly. It was faint, but the arms and legs sticking out of his way-too-small Plutonian jersey were a distinct shade of blue. "He's definitely blue."

"They gened him," Venetio marveled. "The Plutonians gened him!"

For a split second, I was angry. How could they?

But then I saw the smile on Elliot's face. And I realized that if he had indeed been gened, it must have been his idea. And it didn't look like he regretted it.

"Elliot, what have you done?" I muttered, just as the bone-rattling sound of the gong rang out once again.

"Oh my goodness, the second sudden death period has begun!"

The firewalls rose again around the field. This time, they were so high I could barely see Elliot.

"Never in history has the second sudden death period come so soon after the first!" the announcer was screaming, a scrap of tortilla dangling from his lower lip. *"This is unprecedented! This is unbelievable!"*

"This is bad," Venetio muttered, his cheek flat against the window. "Really bad."

"What?" I asked, tearing my eyes away from the Jumbotron. "Why is it bad?"

Venetio gestured down to the crowd. Everybody wearing blue— scratch that, everybody who *was* blue—was shouting up at the box.

"Two sudden death periods back to back? That never happens," Venetio explained. "They think you rigged it."

"Me?" I asked, incredulous.

"Well, they think somebody rigged it," Venetio explained. "If the Martians win during a questionable sudden death period—"

"Stop the game!" I said, quietly at first. Then I turned toward Ms. Helen and raised my voice. "Stop the game!"

"You can't—" she began.

"I'm the chancellor!" I yelled. "I'm the chancellor, and I say, *Stop the game!*"

"Nobody can stop the game during sudden death," she said. "It's against the rules."

I opened my mouth to argue with her, but I was interrupted by a hysterical burst from the announcer's booth.

"It's Tycho Brawn on a breakaway!"

I stared down at the field with dread. Tycho Brawn was charging down the field behind the flaming ball. The close-up shot of him on the Jumbotron showed a grotesque plastic nose and a face that was filled with determination. A determination to end the game, once and for all. In a way that would give the BURPSers exactly what they wanted.

And the only thing between him and the vast Plutonian goal was Elliot.

The Return of the Phenom

It's a showdown!" the announcer screeched as Tycho Brawn came barreling toward the Plutonian goal. "*A trial by fire, literally, for the new Plutonian goalie! With the entire game on the line! The fate of their planets is in the hands of these two players!*"

The announcer thought he was being dramatic. He had no idea that he was right.

"Come on, Elliot!" I yelled at the window, completely forgetting that I was supposed to be neutral. "*Come on!*"

"Tycho always shoots right," Sylvie muttered, her voice tense. "If Elliot's been paying attention, he'll know that Tycho always shoots high and to the right. High and right, Elliot! High and right!"

"High and right!" Sylvie, Venetio, and I yelled. "High and right!"

I don't know if he heard us. Really, there was no way he could have. Not from behind a closed, bulletproof window hundreds of meters above his head. Maybe he didn't need to hear us. But when

Tycho Brawn's shot came sailing at the goal, Elliot jumped, arms outstretched, high and to the right.

The ball hit his gloves. Elliot snatched the ball out of the air and fell on top of it, smothering the flames.

Tycho Brawn stood over him, furious. His face on the Jumbotron looked murderous.

The Plutonians in the stands erupted in cheers as the Plutonian ref jogged over and stood pointedly over Elliot, staring Tycho Brawn straight in the face.

The big Martian backed off and stalked back to midfield in a huff.

The Plutonians in the crowd were still shouting, but not at the chancellors' box. Now they were focused on the lanky, blueish figure in front of the Plutonian goal. They were smiling.

And they were chanting: "Foster! Foster! Foster!"

"The sudden death period is over! Just four minutes of regular time remain!"

I took a very deep breath and looked over at Sylvie.

"So…that's why you don't play anymore?" I guessed. "Because of what happened in the '14 Finals?"

She nodded.

"It was all a lie," she said. "We didn't win; we cheated. We were all famous for no reason."

"You didn't cheat," I pointed out.

"No, but I knew Tycho did. And I didn't tell anybody."

"That's why you don't play anymore?"

"That's right."

"Sylvie," I gulped, as I snuck a look at the game clock: three fifty-five. "You can make up for that now. You can win this game for the Martians right now."

"I'm not playing, Sawyer," she said.

"Hmmm," I said with a glance at Venetio. "Yeah, I guess you wouldn't make much of a difference anyway."

"Yeah," Venetio said casually. "I doubt Coach Kepler would even let her play."

"He's been begging me to play since I got here," Sylvie corrected him testily.

"Plus, she hasn't played for a while," I pointed out. Venetio and I both turned our backs on her, but not before I saw her mouth drop open in shock. I bit back a grin.

"She's probably not very good anymore," Venetio said thoughtfully.

"Totally out of shape," I added.

"Has-been," Venetio sniffed.

"Plus, she's short," I pointed out.

Venetio snorted. "I mean, sure she got a few goals past Elliot the other day. But she's no match for professional Plutonian players. Not anymore."

"It's better if she doesn't play," I agreed. "I mean, let's face it. She was on the '14 Finals team, and apparently they had to cheat to beat the Plutonians, so…"

I risked a glance over my shoulder, wondering if we needed to go even further.

But we didn't. Sylvie's seat was empty.

"Short?" Venetio repeated, raising an eyebrow.

I nudged him in the ribs.

"Sometimes, you've just got to know what buttons to push."

"Ladies and gentlemen, substitution for the Martians. Number twenty-two, Sylvia Juarez, has taken the field!"

"With the score still at 0–0, the fiery phenom has returned! But with only two minutes left in regulation time, will she make a difference?"

"What happens if she doesn't score a goal?" I asked Venetio, pressing my face against the glass as I tried to get a better view of the game.

"It'll go into a shoot-out," Venetio answered. "Two players, one from each team, alternate shots on goal until somebody scores. Both teams have preselected the players who will represent them."

"Let me guess, the Martians chose Tycho Brawn?" I asked.

Venetio nodded. "And he'll miss on purpose. The Plutonians will win."

"Come on, Sylvie!" I shouted.

It didn't last long. The Plutonians lost the ball around midfield, and the Martians passed it to Brawn, who started charging downfield toward Elliot again. It was only a matter of time before he pretended to trip, lose the ball, or miss. Just like he had been doing the whole game, when it wasn't sudden death.

Except that this time Tycho Brawn had a small, red-jerseyed blur on his tail.

"Sylvia Juarez is keeping pace with Brawn! Is this a new offense they've

been cooking up? Maybe—wait! Is she... She is! Sylvia Juarez is trying to steal the ball from her own teammate!"

Sylvie kicked the ball right out from between Tycho Brawn's legs. The bigger player roared, got tangled up in his own feet, and fell over.

"No foul! Both refs are saying no foul! Sylvia Juarez is clear to the goal!"

The Jumbotron camera moved from Brawn, who was lying on the ground and beating the grass with his fists, to Sylvie's resolute face to Elliot...who stood shaking in front of the goal.

I'm not sure if it happened in slow motion for everybody else, but it was definitely that way for me. Sylvie drew back her foot and the ball seemed to inch toward the goal. Elliot jumped and flew, arms outstretched, high and right.

The ball sailed by him, low and left, into the goal, just as the buzzer signaling the end of the game sounded. The final score flashed across the Jumbotron:

Martians: 1

Plutonians: 0

The stadium erupted in cheers.

"SYL-VI-A!" the Martians in the crowd were chanting. "SYL-VI-A! SYL-VI-A!"

"SYL-VI-A!" echoed Venetio, beating his hands together. When he caught me looking at him, he gave an embarrassed smile.

"I never thought I'd be rooting for the Martians," he said, wiping away a tear.

"You know what, Venetio? Neither did I."

Down on the field, Sylvie was helping a prostrate Elliot to his feet. She looked up at the box and gave me a small salute with her free hand.

I knew what she meant, and I felt the tension that had momentarily lifted settle back down on my shoulders.

They had done it. Mars had won the game. Fair and square.

Now it was my turn.

Wherein I Save the Planet

L adies and gentlemen, it's now time to vote," I said gravely, standing at the head of the table and facing the twelve members of the Martian Council. I handed a stack of paper ballots to the Martian on my right. "The question you must decide today is whether or not to ban the Plutonians from the Intergalactic Soccer Federation."

Twelve heads nodded in agreement. They all looked bored. Not like they were about to debate and argue about an important decision.

Which means that Elliot had probably been right—they already knew exactly how they were going to vote.

"Just out of curiosity," I mused, "has everyone here already made up their minds?"

The old Martian at the head of the table cleared his throat irritably.

"Son," he said to me. "I think we all know how this is going to go. The Plutonians must be taught a lesson. Let's just get it over with, shall we?"

"Do you all feel that way?" I asked the table.

There were nods all around.

"I was afraid of that," I said. "Which is why I made sure that the tacos you ate earlier contained a secret ingredient to help you make the right choice."

"A—a what?" the old Martian asked, exchanging puzzled glances with the Martian across from him.

"A secret ingredient," I repeated. Then I took a deep breath. "I'm afraid you have all been gened."

Twelve mouths dropped open in shock.

"Gened?" the old Martian exclaimed. "With what DNA?"

"Plutonian," I said pleasantly.

The old Martian laughed.

"If you think for one second that we're going to believe—"

"*Aughhh!*"

Chancellor Fontana jumped up from her seat. There was a look of pure horror on her face as she stared down at her arm…which was now sporting a distinctively blue smear of color from her wrist, all the way to her elbow.

"It's happening!" she screamed.

"You should all begin showing symptoms within the next hour or so," I informed them.

"Wait a second," the old Martian growled, pointing a bony finger at me. "You ate one of those tacos too. I saw you."

"Yes, I did," I admitted. "Which is why I'm very glad to say that there is good news for all of us."

I motioned to the door. Mrs. Juarez entered, holding another tray of steaming foil packets.

"Hello again," she said cheerfully, grinning at the horrified Martians around the table.

"The tacos we ate contained a virus that was injected with a fast-replicating form of Plutonian DNA," I explained as I took one of the foil-wrapped packets off the tray. "These tacos contain the cure, a second virus that will completely neutralize the first. All you have to do to get one of the cure tacos is vote no on the Plutonian ban."

Very pointedly, I unwrapped my taco and took a huge bite.

"Delicious," I enthused, swallowing. "I feel better already."

"This is blackmail," the old Martian snarled.

"Maybe," I said, licking cheese sauce from my fingers. Then I dropped my casual act and addressed the table very seriously.

"I think we all know this decision is about more than just soccer. You are all free to vote however you like, of course. But when you do, you will be making your choice as Plutonians. This was the only way I could think of to make you see things from someone else's point of view."

The Martians all exchanged nearly identical looks of shock. But I could see the thoughts racing behind their eyes. Thoughts they had never had before. What they would look like when their skin turned blue. What it would be like, never being able to root for their soccer team again. How it would feel to live on a cold, distant non-planet at the mercy of more powerful planets who didn't like them.

They would probably never know what it was really like to be a Plutonian. But for a few minutes at least, I had made them see the world just a little bit differently. I had made it personal.

I was pretty sure Harriet the polar bear would have been proud of me.

I grinned, swallowed, and crumpled my empty taco wrapper in one hand.

"Now, who needs a pen?"

"Congratulations," said Elliot sometime later when we were alone in the box. "You saved Mars."

"So did you," I pointed out. "And so did Sylvie."

"Yeah, well, you were the only one actually trying to do it."

"You couldn't have known," I said. "You left before Venetio told us what the BURPSers were going to do."

"Well, I'm glad I didn't mess up your plan," he said, stretching one of his faintly blue arms out in front of him. "I should have listened to you when you said you had one."

His eyes drifted over to the taco tray. Exactly thirteen of them had been eaten. But Mrs. Juarez had made a few extras.

"So…will those 'cure' tacos work on me too?" Elliot asked.

"Actually…there wasn't a cure in any of those tacos," I admitted. "Because there wasn't a virus in the first batch."

Elliot nodded knowingly.

"I thought so. I mean, I didn't think you'd really gene anybody."

"I'm glad the Martian Council didn't know that," I said. "We definitely fooled them. We were lucky that Chancellor Fontana turned out to be such a good actress."

And also that a mixture of some of Mrs. Juarez's eye shadows had produced the right shade of blue to smear all over her arm.

"So…there's no cure?" Elliot asked.

"I'm sorry, there isn't," I said, looking closely at Elliot's eyes. He had seemed happy to be part Plutonian, but it had been impossible to tell for sure on the Jumbotron. "Not one that works. Not yet anyway."

Elliot shrugged.

"That's OK. I'm not sure I'd take it anyway. It was my choice to get gened. Being part Plutonian isn't so bad. Coach Charon even offered me a spot on the Plutonian team!"

"That's awesome!" I guess Elliot had made the traveling team after all. He'd have to travel a bit farther than just the next county over, but still.

"And I guess I'll have to think of a way to cover the blue at school," he added thoughtfully.

"You should talk to Ms. Helen about that," I suggested.

"Good idea."

"Hey, where did Sylvie go?"

Elliot smirked.

"She's down on the field, greeting her adoring fans. Signing autographs and stuff."

I raised an eyebrow.

"Don't tell me she *likes* being famous now."

Elliot shrugged. "I'll never figure that girl out."

I wasn't sure I ever would either. But I suppose it's easier to enjoy getting attention when you know you really deserve it.

I gestured to the tray.

"Do you want some of the extra tacos? They may not cure anything, but they're delicious."

"No thanks," Elliot said. "I'm still pretty full from the Nutri Juice I drank during the toast. Ms. Helen was right—it isn't too bad! Way better than Bruno egg whites anyway!"

Elliot left after that, and as he did, my grandfather limped through the door.

"Oh wow," I said.

He had been pretty quiet during the game, mostly staying hidden underneath his trench coat. And now I understood why. Over the past couple of hours, his dinosaur parts had grown back almost completely. The back of his shirt was in shreds. His plates, from his neck to his tailbone, were the size of large dinner plates. His tail reached all the way to the ground, and even though the four spikes at the end were still stubs, they were already sharp enough to dig themselves into the carpet behind him.

"Ouch!" he exclaimed, stopping in the doorway to yank his spikes free.

"Wow," I said again.

He set his tail back down and walked all of the way into the room. I cringed as his spikes dug into the carpet behind him again.

"Well, I did promise you an adventure, didn't I?"

"Yes, you did," I remembered. "Hey, have you heard anything about Sunder Labs yet?"

"I just spoke with the Martian police," he said. "They blasted into the lab about a half hour ago. Dr. Marsh and Sylvie's dad have both been arrested. And with their help, the police were able to arrest all of the BURPSers in Mars and confiscate the gene-ing materials that were meant for the water supply."

I nodded. I wondered how Sylvie was going to take that news.

My grandfather squeezed my shoulder.

"Sylvie will be fine," he said, reading my thoughts. "She has her mom. And you and Elliot."

"And Mrs. Juarez has you," I said, smiling mischievously up at him.

"Um, yes. She does," he mumbled. And I could have sworn his cheeks turned a little bit pink. He cleared his throat.

"For the record, I was wrong about this not being our problem. I think you knew that all along, and you were right to take it on. Who knows? Maybe the Plutonians just needed to know that not everybody is against them. Maybe now that they know there's somebody on their side, they'll get the BURPSers under control themselves. And maybe the Martians will give them more of a chance."

"You think?" I asked.

He motioned to the window.

"See for yourself."

I looked down at the stadium. Most of the seats were still filled with a sea of red- and blue-jerseyed fans. They were all sitting unnaturally still. Everyone was staring up at the Jumbotron where someone had turned on MBC-E.

"What's everyone watching?" I asked.

"The season finale of *The Big Bang Theory*," my grandfather replied. "The Martian police were sure there was going to be trouble as soon as the council voted to boot the Plutonians out of the ISF. When that didn't happen—thanks to you—nobody really knew what to do with themselves. Then Chancellor Fontana remembered the finale was on tonight, so they put it up on the big screen."

"Amazing! Sylvie's dad was right!" I said as the whole stadium erupted into laughter over a shared joke. I saw a Martian doubled over in giggles, holding on to the shoulder of a nearby Plutonian for support. Next to them, I saw a Plutonian split a Nutri Nugget in half and give a chunk to his Martian neighbor. Behind them, two Martians and a Plutonian clinked their bottles of Nutri Juice together in a toast.

"Right about what?" my grandfather asked.

I grinned.

"Nothing has united the galaxy like a shared love of American TV."

My grandfather put his hand on my shoulder.

"Speaking of home, the *Lost Beagle* is fully repaired and ready to take us back to Earth," he said. "Let's round everybody up and get out of here, shall we?"

"Yes, let's!" I said wholeheartedly. Suddenly, home sounded like the best idea ever.

We turned toward the door and both grimaced.

There was an enormous gash in the carpet. From the doorway right to the tip of my grandfather's tail spikes.

I sighed. "We've really got to get you some tennis balls," I said.

"Those actually work?"

"Come on, Grandpa," I said, putting my arm around him. "Let's go home."

The Confession

We had missed three days of school, but since my grandfather had told Principal Kline that we'd spent the time volunteering in his research lab, our absences were excused. And as for the wild stories about polar bears and the three of us disappearing in a UFO... Well, according to Principal Kline, the company the school had hired to take care of the cricket problem had sprayed the wrong chemical into the classroom ceilings.

Judging from the continued chirps, not a single cricket had died. But dozens of students and a few teachers had reported symptoms ranging from headaches to memory loss to full-blown hallucinations. Luckily, there didn't seem to be any permanent damage. Except for three basketball hoops mysteriously falling over...

Elliot adjusted fairly easily to his new reality as part Plutonian. Ms. Helen took him to Sephora and taught him how to apply makeup on his face, arms, and legs.

"I wasn't really sure how I felt about that," Elliot admitted.

"The makeup?" I asked.

"No, the makeup is actually sort of fun," he admitted. "But it feels weird to hide the blueness. Like I'm ashamed of it or something. I'm not—I'm proud to be part Plutonian! But Ms. Helen says we have to play it cool for a while, at least until Earthlings are officially told about aliens. Until then, I guess it'll be like I have a secret identity or something! And that's pretty cool, right?"

"Pretty cool," I agreed.

Sylvie presented Elliot with a handmade cold suit modeled after Venetio's. (He'd promised to bring Elliot a real one when he came to visit next month.) It was basically a vest made out of wet suit material that fit underneath clothes and had special compartments to hold ice packs.

Sylvie's mom helped her with the project. They seemed to be getting along a lot better. And now that Sylvie's dad was in a Martian prison, he no longer had an excuse not to answer her emails. They talked more in the first few days after we got home than they had in months. Sylvie said he was very sorry for what he and Sunder Labs had almost done and was determined to make amends.

I was reserving judgment on Mr. Juarez, but Sylvie seemed happy. And that's what mattered most.

Unfortunately, our time away had not had any effect on the stalemate between Orlando and Ms. Filch. When the lunch bell rang on our first day back at school, no one even looked toward the door. Everybody just remained in their chairs and took out their lunches without Ms. Filch having to say anything. And judging by the determined looks on both of their faces, neither Orlando nor Ms. Filch were close to budging.

This went on for four more days. Finally, when the lunch bell rang on our fifth day back home, I stood up.

"Ms. Filch? I'd like to confess."

"Sawyer," she said gently, "I know you weren't the one who put glue on my chair. Please sit down."

"But you said that a confession is about more than just who did it. It's about taking responsibility. And I'd like to do that. I'll accept whatever punishment you think is fair."

Ms. Filch gave me a very long look.

"Are you sure, Sawyer?" she asked finally.

"I'm sure," I said.

"And no one else has anything to say about this?" she prodded, staring straight at Orlando.

Nobody, including Orlando, said anything.

"All right," she said finally. "Then I accept your confession, Sawyer. We'll discuss your punishment later. For now, you and the rest of the class are excused to go outside for the rest of the lunch period."

Most of the class needed no prompting to jump out of their seats and head for the door. I took my time and packed up my salad slowly. When I was done, the only people left in the room were me and Ms. Filch.

"I'm a bit confused, Sawyer," she said, looking genuinely puzzled as she leaned against the desk in front of mine. "Why would you do that?"

I shrugged. I couldn't exactly tell Ms. Filch that a pair of polar bears and a Plutonian soccer enthusiast had made me feel differently about people who sat by themselves at lunch every day. So I just said: "Someone has to do something. Why shouldn't it be me?"

Ms. Filch nodded thoughtfully and crossed her arms.

"From what I hear, this isn't the first time you've fought for someone who may or may not have deserved your help," she said.

I drew in a quick breath. For a second, I thought she somehow knew all about what had happened in Mars. I wondered how she had found out. And whether she thought it was the Martians or the Plutonians (or both) that didn't deserve to be helped.

"I'm talking about the situation last semester," she said, interrupting my thoughts. "I'm still not totally clear on what happened—none of us are, it's all kind of hazy—but from what I understand, you went out of your way to help Allan, Cici, and a bunch of other classmates who hadn't exactly been kind to you."

I spread my hands.

"They needed help," I said. It sounded like a pretty lame explanation for why I had done it, but that was all I could come up with.

"And now Orlando…" Ms. Filch prompted me.

I shrugged and spread my hands.

"Maybe he just needs to know there's somebody on his side."

"Perhaps," Ms. Filch said. She sounded doubtful. I guess she must have really liked those jeans. "I'm not sure about Orlando, Sawyer. But it sounds to me like you might have found your passion."

"My passion?" I echoed, as a wave of panic washed over me. I was pretty sure I had left my Possible Passions list somewhere in the Juarezes' apartment in Mars.

Ms. Filch winked at me.

"Just in time too. Your paper is due tomorrow."

Orlando was waiting for me right outside the classroom door.

"No one believes you did it," he told me flatly. "I already posted that picture on Instagram, and all of the details are up on my blog."

"I know that," I said. "It wasn't about taking credit. And it was just a one-time thing, by the way. The next time you do something that gets everybody in trouble, you're on your own. And we'll all be back having to eat lunch at our desks."

He narrowed his eyes at me as though *I* might be pranking *him*.

"Or," I continued, "maybe tomorrow you could skip the pranks and sit at our table for lunch."

"Your table?" he asked, and he stared at me for so long that his glasses slipped down the length of his nose.

"Yeah," I told him. "You can't miss it—it's right by the bathroom. See you there."

The next day at lunch, Elliot, Sylvie, and I all arrived at our table together.

When I opened my backpack to take out my salad, my paper, "Sticking Up for People Who Need It," peeked out. Elliot reached down and swiped it before I could stop him.

"You finished it!" he exclaimed, then pointed excitedly to the large A Ms. Filch had written in the upper right-hand corner. "And you beat Sylvie!"

I grinned. Even without the help of my brainstorming list, it had been surprisingly easy to write the paper last night. I had turned it in that morning and been shocked when Ms. Filch graded it before lunch.

"Actually, we tied," Sylvie said, pulling a paper out of her bag and slapping it down on the table. Right beside the title, "Getting Through It When a Parent Lets You Down," was a large A. "Given recent events, I thought my initial topic needed some revision. I turned in a new paper this morning."

"Maybe I should rewrite mine too," Elliot said, then made a face. "But if Ms. Filch doesn't think basketball is a good enough passion, I doubt she'd feel any differently about soccer. She just doesn't understand sports!"

I nodded sympathetically, but my eyes kept drifting over toward Orlando's usual lunch table. It was empty.

"Do you think he'll come?" I asked.

"I didn't hear about any shenanigans happening this morning," Sylvie said, pulling a Ziploc bag out of her front pocket. "Maybe that means that he—"

"What is that?" Elliot exclaimed, pointing at Sylvie's bag. I don't think he could have looked more surprised if she had pulled out a large snake.

"It's a sandwich," Sylvie said pleasantly, taking an enormous bite of the object in question. Then, when we both continued to stare at her, she added, her mouth still full, "You know, two pieces of bread with stuff in between? I thought you guys would know about it. It's sort of an Earth thing."

"We know what it is," Elliot sputtered. "I just didn't think you—holy cow, are those sprouts? What happened to all the candy?"

Sylvie swallowed.

"I'm in training," she informed him. "I may only be a part-time Razer now because of school and stuff, but if we're going to make it to the finals this year, I need to be on top of my game. Eating too much sugar is really bad for you, you know."

Elliot's mouth dropped open in shock. I stifled a laugh. And someone else nearby cleared his throat.

"Um, hi," said Orlando, holding a blue zippered lunch sack out in front of him like a shield.

"Hi," I said, nudging an empty chair toward him with my foot. "You know Sylvie and Elliot, right?"

"I remember Elliot," Orlando said, sitting gingerly and setting his sack on the table. He turned to Sylvie. "But you're new this year, right?"

"Yup," she answered, swallowing. "I read your blog. It's pretty good. But remind us to tell you about the time we broke into the administration building in the middle of the night."

Orlando's eyes bulged.

"Seriously? The three of you did that?"

"What? Don't we look like the types?" Elliot asked, grinning. Then he absentmindedly scratched a spot on his arm, leaving a slightly blue streak of skin peeking through his makeup.

Orlando didn't seem to notice. He just opened his lunch sack and pulled out a large plastic container.

My tail twitched at the smell of fresh greens.

"Is that a salad?" I asked.

He nodded, looking slightly embarrassed. "Yeah. Salad's my favorite. It's kind of weird, I know…"

"Orlando," I said, "if there's one thing I've learned this year, it's that weird is pretty relative."

I tipped my Tupperware bowl toward him so he could see the contents. Then I raised my fork.

After a moment's hesitation, he raised his own fork and clinked it against mine.

"Glad you could join us, Orlando," I said.

"Me too. Call me Lando."

Author's Note

First off, in the Author's Note to *Dinosaur Boy*, I said there were some hints in that book about where the series would be headed next, but that I would save my explanations for the second Dinosaur Boy book. Now I can tell you there were three clues:

1. Sawyer's school is called Jack James Elementary School. Jack James was the project manager of the Mariner 4 mission, which took the first pictures of Mars.
2. The security guard who almost busts Sawyer, Elliot, and Sylvie when they are breaking into the school is from Viking Security. That was a reference to the Viking landers, which went to Mars in the 1970s.
3. In Chapter 8, when Dr. Cook is talking about the science fair, he tells the kids that it's "the perfect opportunity for you to really get into the spirit of the scientific method" and

also to "[l]et your curiosity run wild!" That wasn't just good advice: *Spirit* and *Opportunity* are both the names of rovers that landed on Mars in 2004, and *Curiosity* is a mobile science lab that arrived in 2012.

The research for the Dinosaur Boy books is always ridiculously fun, and this one was no exception. The history of space exploration is full of amazing stories, extremely smart and interesting people, and exciting visions about our future as a species. I had a blast sneaking in references to some of the fun stuff I found whenever I could.

Venetio Lowell was named for Venetia Burney, the eleven-year-old girl who named Pluto. In 1930, when Venetia's grandfather (an Oxford University librarian) told her that a new planet had been discovered, she told him they should name it "Pluto" after the Roman god of the underworld. Her suggestion eventually made it all the way to the astronomers at Lowell Observatory, who chose it as the planet's official name.

Sawyer's grandfather, Dr. Franklin, was named in honor of Rosalind Franklin, a pioneering woman of science whose part in the discovery of the double-helix structure of DNA went largely unacknowledged during her lifetime. (Three men were awarded the Nobel Prize for this discovery in 1962, four years after Franklin's death).

Ms. Helen's last name, "Tombaugh," is a tribute to Clyde Tombaugh, the astronomer who discovered Pluto in 1930 while working at the Lowell Observatory. The *New Horizons* spacecraft reportedly carried some of Tombaugh's ashes as it cruised by Pluto and sent back photos in July 2015.

The various chancellors on Mars are all named for individuals who made some of the earliest telescope observations of Mars:

Chancellor Fontana was named for Francesco Fontana, an amateur astronomer who used a handmade telescope to make observations (and woodcut drawings) of Mars in the 1630s.

Chancellor Gio was named after Giovanni Schiaparelli, an Italian astronomer whose discovery of crisscrossing *canali* ("channels" in Italian) on the surface of Mars in the 1870s was incorrectly translated into English as "canals." This led to a hugely popular theory that there were intelligent, canal-building life-forms on Mars. Although ultimately disproved (unless Sylvie's right and the Martians are just messing with us), the theory continues to spark people's imaginations today.

Chancellor Gale was named for Walter Frederick Gale, an Australian banker who observed Mars with a telescope he built himself in the late 1800s. The Gale Crater, where *Curiosity* landed in 2012, was also named for him (although not by me!).

I chose the name "Asaph" for Sylvie's dad after Asaph Hall, the astronomer who discovered Mars' two moons, Phobos ("horror") and Deimos ("terror").

Tycho Brawn was named for Tycho Brahe, a famously eccentric astronomer known for his accurate measurements. The Tycho in this book wore a fake nose because he lost his in a gene-ing attempt. The real Tycho wore a fake nose because he lost part of his in a duel over a math equation. Tycho Brahe died after a lengthy banquet in Prague where, depending on who you ask, he was either murdered or having such a good time that he forgot to go to the bathroom, which caused his bladder to burst. He also might have helped inspire Shakespeare's *Hamlet.* You can't make this stuff up.

The *Sabatier,* the small spaceship Sawyer and his friends rent, is named for the Sabatier reaction, a chemical process that produces methane and water from carbon dioxide and hydrogen. Since this is a relatively simply way to produce both water and rocket fuel, some people (notably Robert Zubrin in his book *The Case for Mars*) theorize that this reaction may become important for eventual human colonization of Mars.

The Kuiper Kickers (K2) got their name from the Kuiper Belt, an area of the solar system beyond Neptune that includes Pluto and at least two other so-called "dwarf planets": Haumea and Makemake. The Kickers' Coach Charon is named for Pluto's largest moon. Their goalie, "Stern," is named for Alan Stern, the principal investigator of NASA's New Horizons mission to Pluto.

Orlando Eris was named partly for Lando Calrissian (the reformed smuggler and friend of Han Solo in Star Wars) and partly for Eris, the largest dwarf planet in our solar system. The discovery of Eris in 2005 (and the fact that it is bigger than Pluto) was one of the major reasons the International Astronomical Union decided to officially define the three qualifications for being a planet (which caused Pluto to be reclassified as a dwarf planet).

Coach Kepler, the coach of Mars's Red Razers, is named for Johannes Kepler. He started out as Tycho Brahe's assistant and is most well-known for identifying Kepler's laws of planetary motion.

The players on the Martian soccer team are all named for various individuals who are actively involved in furthering our understanding of Mars today: Bruce Jakosky (principal investigator of NASA's MAVEN mission to study the Martian atmosphere); William Banerdt (project leader for InSight, NASA's planned 2016 mission to study the interior geology of Mars); Dr. K. Radhakrishnan (the chairman of the Indian Space Research Organization, whose Mars Orbiter mission put a craft into orbit around Mars in 2014); and Robert Zubrin, an author and aerospace engineer whose inspiring enthusiasm for a manned mission to Mars can't be denied.

The *Lost Beagle* got its name from *Beagle 2*, a British spacecraft launched in 2003 as part of the Mars Express mission. It lost contact on December 25, 2003, just before it was supposed to land on Mars. Its fate was a big mystery until 2014, when images of *Beagle 2* were finally transmitted (the spacecraft having landed successfully but with a malfunctioning communications antenna) by NASA's Mars Reconnaissance Orbiter.

The lizards that produced the eggs for the really gross omelet and the '14 Finals toast are called "Brunos" after Giordano Bruno, an Italian thinker who was burned at the stake in 1600 for (among other things) his controversial view that there might be life on other planets. The SETI (Searching for Extra-Terrestrial Intelligence) League gives an award every year called "the Bruno" to honor significant contributors to their field.

And the dinosaur with the crested head that Sawyer thinks he sees as they're taking off from Saturn? That's a *Corythosaurus*, of course. It's always been my favorite dinosaur. I have no idea why…

Much love and galaxy-sized hugs,

CPO

Acknowledgments

My dinosaur-kid-in-space odyssey wouldn't have been possible without the help of the following wondrous people, all of whom I owe a batch of homemade Nutri Nuggets (at the very least):

My fantastic agent, Sarah LaPolla, for *getting it* and for always having my back.

My wonderful editor, Aubrey Poole. (I'm looking forward to our queso date!) Fantastic production editor Elizabeth Boyer, incredible copy editor Diane Dannenfeldt, fabulous page designer Nesli Anter, and genius cover artist Marek Jagucki. Ace publicist Kathryn Lynch. Marketing wizards Alex Yeadon and Beth Oleniczak. Sourcebooks library superstar, Jean Johnson. And everybody else at Sourcebooks, for giving the Dinosaur Boy books a perfect home.

Tara Costello, Chrissy Costello, and Cameron Wilson for helping me come up with Orlando's pranks (and then screening them for believability and coolness).

Jordan Womack for educating me on soccer-football terminology.

Steve Richardson and Derek Sawyer, the two most patient geologists of my acquaintance, for putting up with questions like, "What type of rock would make a Martian miner cry?" and follow-ups like "Yeah, but can you think of one with a cooler-sounding name?"

The late Carl Sagan, for writing *Cosmos*. Also Ann Druyan, Pam Abbey, and everybody at Druyan-Sagan Associates for giving me permission to use my favorite *Cosmos* quote at the beginning of this book.

The creators of Star Wars, *The Big Bang Theory*, and *Doctor Who*, for inspiring various parts of this book.

The entire Kid Lit writing community of Austin, Texas, with extra-special thanks to Cynthia Leitich Smith, Greg Leitich Smith, Mari Mancusi, Nikki Loftin, P. J. Hoover, and Jo Whittemore.

Jane Vaughn and Kim Delinski, for keeping me (relatively) sane on a daily basis.

You! For picking up this book and making it all the way to the Acknowledgments section. (Woo-hoo!)

And most of all, my wonderful family: Mark, Sophia, and Alex, for taking this incredible adventure with me and for continuing to love me, even when I'm on deadline and certifiably insane. I love the three of you to Pluto and back, times a billion.

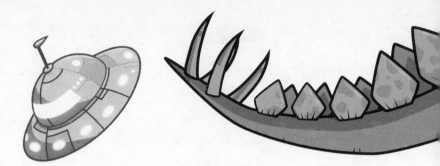

About the Author

Cory Putman Oakes earned her BA (in psychology) from the University of California at Los Angeles and her JD from Cornell Law School, and then naturally decided to pursue a profession that utilized neither of these. Her first book (*The Veil*, a young adult novel) was published in 2011, and she has been writing for kids and teens ever since.

When she's not writing, Cory enjoys running, cooking, and hanging out with her husband and kiddos at their home in Austin, Texas. She is often on Twitter (@CoryPutmanOakes) and Facebook. You can find out more about Cory and her books (plus recipes for things like Nutri Nuggets and Mrs. Juarez's molé sauce) on her website, www.corypoakes.com.